Splitting

For Pete

Splitting

Your balloon-to-the-moon
Saves the Day!

Brian Charles Clark

Brian C Clark

Jan. 2000

AQUAKNOWLEDGEMENT

To all those I've playgiarized, thanks for the bang on me hear!
Thanks especially to Dawn Levy for her close and questing
reading. Thanks to all, the quick and the dead, with whom I've
awhile'd and away'd: your love lingers.

Wordcraft of Oregon
P.O. Box 3235
La Grande, OR 97850

Design by Quark Bosch/Soul Horse, San Francisco.

for
CHRISTOPHER MICHAEL CLARK
1960–1997
where the river runs

BARBARUS

I am a stranger here,

HIC EGO

for no one understands me. —Ovid

SUM, QUIA

NON ULLI

INTELLIGOR.

KOH

THE CRUSH FROM THE INJECTION *while supplies last* kicks me in the chest, a chill metal gasp fleeing custody, a lightning of Tartars hording down my medulla oblongata. Compounding chords, like the drone I heard last time we saw the flying saucer. TV induces illiteracy *this week only*. The itch that roils, the feed from the media line, the news waves in like a bath of riffs, the wake-up punch of water bullets, barely seeing the remains of the day before, I'm reel-to-reeling from the effects of the drugs they make me take here. Implanted memory syndrome compresses all experience into a singularity, and time, coming to burn the village, crumbles like the plaster face of a false idol.

Neocortex-penetrating carrier waves are generated with moiré patterns, waves so dense with information the entire *Opus Contra Naturum* can be limned in just a few microwatts. Which is exactly what the aliens have instituted, although I admit this is not a very popular idea.

It's because of the microdots. All colors are separated into just six colors and these six are recombined in stochastic arrays of tiny dots all along the radium shower. Warp and woof—optical illusion, Goethe reminds, is optical truth. The scan lines of television are a weaver's flying hands. Based on the matrix, the telepathic expression of the feminine, consciousness is holographic, and the patient can only digress. Making me an engine of bifurcatory profusion, a seeker beside myself, salted with desire.

Try to remember what we must have known. In this sweating knitting prison suspended in the static of the TV dream, the gnomic bits are all that survive.

Consciousness is a bird, a free-winging metaphor, a spiraling accretion of dialogical stories, and this is where I split up in order to cover more ground. I *and I* know Rose Mountain is a mystical island of psychic reality veiled in a cloud of unknowing and that KOH will curve there like a coil of DNA. We are a flock of birds, gliding over territories and estuaries and tertiaries, seeking him her it, heresies, connubial bliss where the wings join the spine just below the sky.

∘ ∘ ∘

What must we have known?

One night two friends and I broke into the high-school chemistry lab. I wanted to steal the key.

Yucca Valley High was so worried about finding classroom space for its mushrooming population—Yucca, back when, was one of the fastest growing towns in the former Oneirican States—that security was the least of the administration's concerns. Here's a town that had a Whiskerino Contest during Grubstake Days, fur crusts snakes, their self-saluting tintinnabulation of special*ness.* All the men stopped scraping their faces with sharp rocks on a certain date, and six weeks later, whoever'd grown the longest beard won. *Drifting*—but with a heritage of silver and copper mining, you'd think they'd've had a better conception of the kind of people—*I may have forgotten what was being said. I thought Margarine Not Butter was speaking? Does dennybody else look like her? Mine me, it's an allusive mystery,* and miners hadn't worked that rarified desert for over fifty years, not since the silver ran away with the moon. *I was sure I heard her reciting* *something from the Sibylline prophecy. I wish I could turn off the telequarium.*

Just down the highway was Twentynine Palms Marine Corpse base, *hup* (a nasty mercenary habit that, the belch approaching infinity which signifies a sadistic attempt at individuality within the confines of the conformalist fraternity), the world's largest in land and number of occupants, gateway to the world's largest toxic waste dump.

How we really think?

Chopsticks. Kleenex. Pulp comes from somewhen. *Where?* Wood—paper comes from dammed rivers, just like pixels. *Hair stands on end.* Teleprompted men explain, *We are the special offer, everything must go.* Government off the books, as if some sort of invasion simultaneously erased and rewrote history, making the palimpsest new by pulping the original. *Electrical static.* The cat chews so urgently she forgets she's eaten as she swallows. When the bowl is empty, she turns around and squats, like a meatloaf in the middle of the bare tile, and stares me down for more. *We are powerless and have no control.* Paper still has a shred of consciousness because it once lived in a tree. The same would be true of Dr. Sax's cotton underwear, except the tree would be spieling in the shrubish? Now I'm lost in the proverbial where I can't find any trees, just mushroom-sprouting stumps, the final remains of a once globe-encircling forest. There is a table, a cot, a cat, and the wastebasket is always kept empty.

○ ○ ○

I have tried to explain to the various doctors over the years that our only chance is to use neurobardic stragectories in hopes of initiating a cerebral cascade that will shear away the false memories the aliens have accreted in our brains. Over the years, the doctors have responded with syringes of varying size. So instead of fighting in the resistance, I've been busy recovering from drug

addiction. *The scream I hear stings like rays.* The course of
my treatment has left me fragmented, scattered, and with
very poor edge detection, but from the powders, dust and
shards, a fibrillating vision is emerging. The desperados
will find a way to contact their friends.

Dr. Sax has diagnosed my condition as enthymemic
aposiopesis. That I leave the middles and ends out. I
think it's plain old CIS, Chronosynblastic Infindibular
Syndrome, or, as it is now better known, dystemporalexia
compounded with alien mind control. Then again, I have
nothing better to do than sit around and think. Or so I
presume. It is too easy, and too dangerous, to say anything at all.

○ ○ ○

What we took was simple and specific, *my fault.* The
boys were blameless but for being curious and up for ad-
venture. I wanted the big lump of pure potassium that Mr.
Whitwer kept free from oxygen in a tightly sealed jar of
kerosene. *It's not the addiction that kills, it's the habit.* I had
to get my ball. I was impressed into a fugue of electronically excited obsession by his demonstration of potassium's
reactivity with water. He dropped a little pea of kalium
into a beaker of aqua purabelle. Bloom! The display was
pyrofying. The water molecules rushed to pieces, un-
bounded energy heaving up the potassium sux. A flash
caved into my head; the beaker didn't even move.

"Run for it!" I yelled to Steve and the Pale One, and we
scrambled over the chain-link fence that in those days
didn't even have barbed wire, or anything more than six
feet of pure sneaker rung and rise.

We ran from an impending explosion, ran to find our
future, as that's precisely what they take from us. Certain
memories are gone for good, while others, stolen and re-
gurgitated, are implanted in their place. It's like the opposite of an alcoholic blackout. Instead of being awake but

unaware, losing time in a drug-induced trance, I went to sleep one night and got up the next morning ten years later, with perfect recollection of my decadent life. None of it ever happened, I'm only a day older. This is due to broadcasting, not fiction.

∘ ∘ ∘

"Who was your wife?" The Necks always turn a simple question into a drill bit, daggering it at my head.

"Armamentia Bila, of course," I reply plainly. There is no point in beating around the proverbial. Not while there's a goddess left alive.

"Tell us everything you know about her."

"What's to know?" And I haven't, not for years. I've been busy sitting here telling the Necks how little I know of her.

There may be torture. I have no means of verification. Every day is an island, torn free and floating in a sea of malassociated memory fragments. I'm certain some of the memories are mine, but I can't remember the context of their origin to know for sure. I feel as if I've been in the habit of taking the exact same walk along a beach every day for years, but I've never been here before. Another possibility is that for years I've been sitting with a cat in a small hospital cell. The Necks come and go, quit, get fired or pulled up the sux. I can see the shape of the sea that surrounds me, the endless flat reflecting all our faces, the prison wall made of the weakest thing, and the aliens enslaving me in their driftworks.

I know the Necks are using drugs. On me, I mean, though I suppose among themselves as well. I know I would. Some drugs enhance, others erase and make the mind rerecordable. I wake up from the blackouts with a mouth full of burning feathers, blurred vision, head a roaring ocean, body a sack of throbbing fluids.

Basically, though, it is the simple fact of the implants

that makes me suspicious. Who remembers when this fashion of wearing an RCA jack in the neck started? The television is an aquarium for the aliens. They rule from the inside.

∘ ∘ ∘

Square white room. Pears soap. I think I once had a count of how many bars I've used up, but that little slip of paper is not to be found. There are many iterations of the control-freak movie.

They send in Dr. Olympia Sax.

"I'm familiar with your work," I tell her. "I've read your books." *At some indeterminate point in the past,* I think.

"Why indeterminate?" She smiles with telepathic highlights, and pulls out a pocket pad and pen.

"That's a good question." What did she ask me? "I wish I could remember the answer."

She cocks her head. Her face is a nearly perfect oval, though I don't at all see her as abstract. "What did you do yesterday?"

"I can't tell the difference."

"Would you describe your life as a blur?" As her lips phoneme Ur her thick gray curls vibrate and roll in waves o'er her white-coated shoulders.

"I would describe my life now as being drugged and held against my will for something like the past fifteen years."

"Yes," she says thoughtfully, "I see that in your chart." She pushes her glasses up the long bridge of her nose. "Do you have any religious affiliations you'd like to tell me about?"

"I once loved a Jainist, and never should have left her. Her memory is reincarnated in my heart every day. Personally, I consider myself a gnostic Fortean animist, which is a fancy way of saying I'll believe anything if I witness it myself, but not before." I tap the implant in my neck, nod at hers.

Amanuensis Einstein twirls Madonna Curie's panties around his pinkie. But that can't be right. Hypergnosic hallucinations are a side effect of certain mind-control drugs, such as ketamine, served on a gruelingly regular basis as a soup into which the prison chef may well have spit. *Hospital cook.*

"Have you been menstruating regularly?" Her smile twitches. She may be testing me.

"It's a padded cell," I cycle back obliquely, although this is not strictly true.

"I'm going to change your medication immediately and we'll begin the talking cure in the morning. Now, can you tell me your name?"

I feel I can trust her. She wears sensible shoes. Her books have affected me deeply.

"Denny. Scry? Nairbula. Cody? Whatever it says on my chart today."

Dr. Sax nods and stands up.

"I'll see you tomorrow," she says from the door.

"Time will tell," I say.

She closes the door. The cat comes out from beneath the cot.

◦ ◦ ◦

Tony Cross and I once saw an alien ship descend upon Desert Christ Park. This was long before I met Lydia. Armamentia and I had been childhood sweethearts. Or so certain seeming biographical facts can be interpreted. Armamentia once went with me to Desert Christ Park, when I first moved to Yucca. We were twelve. "What do you do?" she asked. "Sit around and watch the rocks crack?" The lesson I take away is that I never learn. There were dozens of statues in the park, constructed of white-washed cement, some quite large. Several had been knocked over in the Landers earthquake, breaking arms off saints and heads off lambs. You could see the chicken-

wire frames. A ship the size of a Frisbee descended and
bathed a nativity scene in gold fire. *Drone of psychic engines.* Tony and I stood by Joseph beseeching his coat and
couldn't move, as if we were gazing through a window
onto an erotic tableau. The craft emitted a brilliant flash,
a blinding light with a sonic kick that felt like a shot of
smack, inexorable and magnanimous.

Years later, a few weeks before her birthday, Lydia made
twenty-thousand dollars on a dope deal. She took me on a
trip. We spent the next six weeks shooting speed, drowning barbiturates with Christian Brothers brandy in hun-
dred-dollar a night hotel rooms. We never turned a TV on
once. We'd been together a couple of months. I had cast
her horoscope and predicted a dramatic future for her. It
wasn't hard: I could see she and her husband were ripping apart as Flika Oswald seduced Lydia's man away.
We picked up everything at hand and tossed it all into the
air: kids, households, mates. Lydia and I burned through
the drugs, and there was drama enough for all. But for
those few weeks we spent driving from motel to motel,
up and down the coast in my old Toyota, I do think she
loved me. We'd squeeze that memory for years, until it
was so thin and dry it became completely transparent, and
was finally carried away, without our heed, on an invisible wind.

○ ○ ○

Wretched arrhythmia, fork and branch, why do I convulsively mimic vomiting? My stomach an alarm, an
aposiopetic entropy locomotive, I am kiltering down a
desert road, vertigoing into every reaching cactus arm.
This is bad, the light seems to descend from above and
fills my head with hot monitors. I am hypersensitive to
cats. To vomiting. What makes me talk this way? *Me?*
Maybe it's just the squelching TV on all the time. I have
the remote, but there's no power button. *Do not remove*

label. Mouche's choking, barfing, food and hair ball. Engineers must consume a sacred diet in order to maintain their moon-key wrenches properly. *Egyptians.* Her name is not Mouche. *Your hair is not brown.* Or maybe I have telepathic elephantiasis, a thousand nights in just one.

I am the novitiate who knows what she cannot know if she is to survive and ergot broth ryefurcate the unsheathed knowledge from the tube, *we scramble like rabbits through the multiple tunnels of the miner's valley*, everything is bellowing at me. *Manhole.* The world is rushing in to fill the void, absorbing all, the perversity of this absurdly star-spangled heaven, habitat of nocturnal malefactors and thieves of the soul. Telegrams from Pandæmonium written by code-cracking nutshell guerillas. *"I've decided to increase the dosage and frequency of your medication."* Dr. Sax thinks she knows what's good for me. The grammatology of icicle locusts. Real medicine, the halls of medicine, uranium chopstick fever gum. I requested they move the television away from the aquarium, to the other side of the common.

"You must avoid potentially dangerous juxtapositions," I chided them. They made me go to my room for the rest of the day. That had to have been at least a week ago. I thought I was somewhere else completely, I thought—

—*Whose thought?*

What did she psign me? Christ said, *Turn the TV off.* That's why I'm screaming, "For Chrissakes, turn the fucken TV *off.*" It's in the Bible, *swear to Aquaknowledge.* The jihad is fought on the borders of Eros and Panasonic. The cat is having a bath, but this, if memory serves, is nothing new.

∘ ∘ ∘

"The damage to the right temporal lobe presents itself with the patient dowsing for meaning, as if pulled along in her thoughts by some unseen force. In conversation, she makes star-

tling leaps, intuitively digressing, but then, amnesically, for-getting she has digressed. Her free association doesn't start until I ask her a question. But not just any question—I asked her if she wanted to eat and she simply went and got her fork and cat. Later, when her cat was in the other room but we were still sitting at the table, I asked her if she could describe her cat. She produced a hijera of volubility."

I don't think Dr. Sax realizes I can suss her thoughts as she writes. I suppose she'll figure it out when she reads me descrying her in my journal.

○ ○ ○

The truth is, it's not what I said that night but what I did. As the words came out of my mouth, I couldn't be-lieve them—it was like watching a storm of bats flee a cave. My brain, driven by fear of the unknown but cer-tain of a dangerous future, mutinied and kidnapped my vocal tract, leaving the nest of my body frozen in bed. When, small and paralyzed, I finally finished speaking, my lover got up and left in tears, and I was unable to stop her. Of what I said, I can't remember a word, and I've searched everywhere. The memory is not lost; it is stolen, or, perhaps more accurately, eaten. I feel it like a missing tooth that refuses to accept its banishment. *Banshee.*

I don't dare speak her name, or even think it, for fear the aliens will sense the telepathic resonances and put the sux on her. *How will you find me?* The Necks would see her as a way to get me to talk about Armamentia Bila. Dr. Sax might help me, but I can't risk talking about her, ever, until I find her, so Dr. Sax will have to help me reach her indirectly, unwittingly, perhaps by lending me a pair of shoes. I'm operating without consent but with a ticket to ride. I have encrypted cognition of my lover in the chemi-cal formula for a radio station: KOH. Which just might ignite the static.

○ ○ ○

This, rather than an evolution of similar but distinct creatures over time, is a convoluted ideogram, an indigenous interpretation born of the electron guns sticking in at my head. Bats smashing windows after I'd thrown meth into the eyes, and acid onto the windshield, of an agent of the bunk squad. The dope he proffered had brought him on his late-night, one last rip-off visit, so I paid him up with his own buffer-cut crystal blown back—a puff across the fingerprinty mirror—into his lazy, closing eyes.

I was enraged by Agent Bunk's underground presence. The last time he'd come around he'd stung me for a telescope I'd stolen out of some grandpa's backyard. As he stumbled to his feet, clawing at his eyes and cursing me sweaty blue, I howled at Bunk, leaping around and swinging my arms like an ape. I ran amok on him, first grabbing down from the high shelf the nitric acid Randy had left in my trust. Well out of reach of children dared by drugs.

Agent Bunk fled, vision burning, down to Armamentia's pad in the Victorian Dive, but his truck sat conspicuously in the middle of the lot. I sped like a dervish, and slupped out quarter-panel sloshes from my gallon jug of nitric acid in paint-curling spurts. I did a ninja kick and shattered the passenger-side window. As I was gushing nitric all over the seats and shift and peddles of his precious fucken truck, he came yelling out, pissed, eyes streaming from the draino speed stinging his face. I splashed the rest of the highly volatile acid onto the hood of his truck, and hurled the empty bottle at his reddening mug. Missed, gallon jug smithereening on the black top, and turned hide to the wind, running back to the safety of my blue-lit rooms.

Agent Bunk jumped into the hot seat of his truck, grabbed the corrosive handle of advanced transportation, and burned rubber for the emergency room.

When he returned, I was dead asleep with the women

after hours of straining vigil. He came back humiliated by the hospital, his brain a hive of furious bees, and bearing a baseball bat. He started swinging, smashing the bay windows of my shooting gallery. I roared out at the agent wearing a mattress as a shield, but his orbiting bat was a whirling purple bruise that cracked like bone. I retreated, cursing him, which only egged him into the beginning of the destruction of the Magellanic apartment building at Fillmore and Baseline Streets. Something slabbed together in concrete depresses the ground there now.

○ ○ ○

"Things I say three times are true."

You are not making sense, Dr. Sax thinks, but does not say. Human flesh is permeable, our senses leak. Just look at the Necks, dirty breathers. Call myself Jezebel for wanting the curium of the world.

Filled with a surplus of meaning, an incantatory, irresistible force which ruptures discursive language, an adept who holds them in her hand is carried by them and is able to fly. *¡Huntell Mayiz cummen. Green, green, green!* The demon Strable translates; is this not the garden of branching quotations? If I could just ride my centaur down Main Street, lead Apollo's cattle in a charge. *Lyre.* At dawn, I sail with the Spinach Ramada. *They brought you here in a bucket, and there were revolving glass doors.* Lydia and I main-lined methylated antigens trying to shunt down the paradigm generator. Fool's gold in them hills, and pyromaniacal last rites, glass breaking everywhere. A cure more toxic than what might kill us.

I had to get it down from the highest shelf. The cat considers jumping, then has a bath. Cream of tartar can be used in many recipes, including, presumably, mind-control drugs and whipped egg-white concoctions. *A rhapsody of swing.* Sometimes, with the televisions and the medications blaring, it's all I can do to muster the focus to put down even one word to the memory of what *is* happening.

○ ○ ○

The night I was slapped awake by an owl in Santa Barbara, I later slept again, my ears ringing with the implications of the wisdom winging from a koan. In a dream that night, time burned away, ceased, though for a long while I thought it had gotten accidentally looped. A seizure in a dream can tear aside the veil between sleep and waking, rip down the spider webs of reason that dictate a difference. Upon introspection, I discovered the aliens, a life form that eats consciousness. My convulsing brain blocked their psychic controllers. I started to recognize the robots who look human but transmit the medial carrier wave beat frequency that has brainwashed us—for millennia. The aliens are routinized, content, and, I realized in my dream, vulnerable to insurgency. When I awoke, I was locked up, charged with creating a temporal disturbance. I had been lying in a gutter in Hilo, talking to myself, corpus derelecti. Cognitive displacement, Dr. Sax calls it, like I've forgotten where I put my keys.

○ ○ ○

With bombful intent I threw a pure potassium baseball into a chlorinated swimming pool. It was a cigarette breakthrough. It was a pillow fight with my mother. It was a victimless attack against an unseen enemy, an explosive light in the darkness, hydrogen igniting the hidden lurker. It was better than hurling video monitors from the tops of tall buildings, better, even, than inserting foul typographics into the ads of empires the minute before they go to print in million-dollar magazines. Or, anyway, better than sitting in county jail rolling the Bible for smoke and playing cards with the air.

Bright in the night of assumptions, the sudden blossom of chemical radiance ripped like broken glass through the lies of history. Unformed identities and possible futures reared up, backlit by the blast. Exposed in luminous silhouette, my life seemed like the experiment of some alien scientist trying to domesticate the complete protein source, so I ran. I ran out into the desert and hid among the cacti and Joshua trees. Somewhere far away I stopped, and stood softly, still as a refugee.

◦ ◦ ◦

Talk, the Necks command. *Screw you*, I reprimand. Although I am terrorized nauseous by ghostly giants and their moldering members *in the congestion of downtown Mayhem*, afraid they'll tear my head off and skull-fuck me *where corpses built a coliseum*. A man with dreadlocks suddenly appeared beside the cat; did I remember to tell Dr. Sax this? He didn't look very substantial, not like a hologram, more like reflections caught in a shower of oil or the falling fragments of a broken mirror. I think he uttered a trio of disyllabic words, and then he clearly said *green* three times.

Language resides in magic most unqualified, quantum chillins, let us give telepathic madres a vox hereinfore, and the ghost of Lucy in the cauldron, subdivide today's news into cells of signification, each a number according to some simple scheme, and cutting across the dithering system palette like ribbons spewing from a victory parade.

Telephone? As a howlist I partake of hellish and godish ringings and know not wherefore I am. It may be Sax playing doctor—she sounds very far away—or it could be the party line. I wanted to find something I'd lost, I had no clue they'd chain me to the wall. *"You know, if we don't tell her the real story, she'll make up one of her own,"* Dr. Sax says to the phone.

Aprés voodoo, mam'selle.

◦ ◦ ◦

Because my chemistry teacher was a terrorist, is what I

tell them, and sometimes people forget they're telepathic. There was a pea of cesium-137 hidden in the double-fist lump of potassium I stole. I figured this out the day I was smoking some grassy knoll with Junie Lunez, the mother-hipped graveyard-shift guard. As the potassium seethed forces with the water in the pool a few grams of radioactive cesium were misted into the air. I don't know about pale Tim and Steve Hix, but I'm dying. *Leaving.* From small peas do big rads grow. I'm partially immune to the implants, I think because of the exposure to the cesium, but if I even mention this fact people get nervous. Afraid of what, is what I'd like to know, afraid of the truth? *Get out of your box.* An open mind is immunity. Sometimes the bullet becomes a portent arcing across the desert sky.

∘ ∘ ∘

The walls are closing in, TV looming like a governess. "Spraying our elevator's a local pastime and by now there are so many layers you can't see the metal." Despite the relentless grinding of sanders, which should eat away the substrate, *this is live footage*, the paint so well bonded to the metal that it grows, layer upon inexorable layer. Let's Janus-face it, a war on anything is a losing war. *So don't borbor where you eat.* There are rumors of cognitive dissonance among the poor. Even the enzymes in mother's spit won't dissolve it.

Everything is paving up. It's on the *Heaven O'Clock News.* The spaces between are shrinking. *We can be different, long as no one sees us and we don't say nutting. Ryediculous!* The Open Mike gang is looking for trouble; they're trying to break into the lab with their pirate tower; they'll make mint toast out of you. Get on with yer bad salves, git outcher harmonicas invaders of Rome, and blow a blues for Kalia. I sit on the roof fiddling with an eraser as the world burns in the grease of a bloated empire. If Aquaknowledge were here she'd spread her legs and her vulva would well a sea of soothing fluids, tempus puget, salty like tears, soul sounding.

"Clearly," she whispers, and launches into a long low laugh that gives Martians hard-ons and California earthquakes enough energy to dampen the deserts. I'm drunk with Aquaknowledge, answering KOH's prayhers. I've been thinking of her lately, from what I can recall. I hope the aliens don't hear me. *Think about something else.*

Some claim cannabis originated in Tanu Tuva, which explains the triangular postage stamps, and also that datura was brought to Earth by beings from Polaris—the Taoists say the beings carried the flower in their hands as they walked between the stars.

○ ○ ○

The phone rings. Does that mean that I've spent too long? But there is no phone, sturgeon riders? *Stern reminders,* the cat's sixth sense. One of the psychiatrists I visited in Calcutta suggested to me that certain metaphors are to some extent dissociated from their origins, and their meanings banned from the conscious mind. She further assured me, however, that if I ventured to suggest in a Benares bazaar who the aliens really are, I would not get away unhurt. Address unknown, I could only shrug and walk in opposite directions, bills left unpaid. A pluralized catachresis cries out, wounded as an angel, glancing at a tangent, this shattered electronic body of our tribe. A tribe ready to dissemble, come down from the hills, watch a little TV, have a few beers, chase the merry pixels into the white noise of steam-rolling entrainment. Strong in-pressure will now be applied.

○ ○ ○

As soon as an idea or image requires expression in the dry form of prose one can be sure it wants to polemicize, to dualize and to offer discrete definitions rather than a field of perception. The intellect, pneumatic one-winged bird, deals from a position of weakness because it demands dogma, and dogma demands defense; and as the samurai know, there exists no such thing as an adequate defense. Slash! and that's the beginning and end of it. Your brain will make a nice soup.

It is too dangerous to write representationally—to write sequential and reasonable journalism. Finally, very little of any importance can be said in that medium since it comes from and directs itself to one area of the consciousness to the exclusion of all others. Only *poetry* (including texts to be read as well as texts to be sung) and *story* can address consciousness as a whole and yield the bifurcatory cascade that will interrupt the aliens' trance mission. *"Unable to maintain a genuine narrative or continuity, displaying the confabulatory delirium of enthymemic aposiopesis, she must literally make herself up at every moment."*

Poetry and story, which vanish like a cycle of cat's cradles into the zero of the circle of logos-thread, can present reality far more effectively than prose. The image, unlike the idea, cannot be defined but must be identified with. The poetic or narrative image is open, like the integrated consciousness, and can go where the body goes. *"For here is a woman who, in some sense, is in a frenzy. The world keeps disappearing, losing meaning, vanishing—and she must seek meaning,* make *meaning, in a desperate way, throwing bridges of meaning over abysses of meaninglessness, the chaos that yawns continually before her."*

How then can I tell the history of those who specifically reject it? *Mare me.* How can I capture the likeness of constantly fleeing shadows, when I myself have fallen into the trap of time, am caught in the talons of history?

I am still haunted by the question: Why, century after century, have humans gathered together to say NO to something? This something has taken ever-changing forms— predominantly alien televisual politics in the last sixty

years, whether we know it or not—but, by the same to-
ken, even our awareness and our protest are fragmented.
This is the first unwritten law of alienation, and we need
to be conscious of it: The something we say NO to is never
the real enemy, but only the shadow it casts over and
within us.

In wine is remembrance. Therefore, we must be drunk
as much as we can, in whatever way we can. When intellect becomes intuition it sheds prose like a snakeskin, and
dons its many colored-coat of poetry. In this sense, art is
necessary because it constitutes the only possible language
of such a rebirth. I feel the rush like someone's showing
me a photograph and I suddenly recall seeing the same
thing once myself, at a decisive moment I have somehow
long before forgotten.

∘ ∘ ∘

My face is changing with every line I leave. I have swal-
lowed granite, and it reproduces inside me. The invasion
of the definitive article is genuine, vaster than empires and
more slow. Martin Buber holds my hand, sitting on a
school boy's chair next to the flotation device. Paradigms
mushroom in a super-saturated warehouse that orbits behind the moon. Pater Buber has already donated one leg
to the osteopoetic Mikhail Bakhtin. *The defensive fragment.*
I am dying in bed, brightness falls from the air. Buber clears
a golem from his throat. The decadent breakdown of the
paragraph, the dismissal of Law as captain of the Ship of
Narrative, the good ship itself tossed to pieces by the pitch
and yaw of necrogenital forces, the vatic disaster or alien
artifice that ended the reich of enlightenment. Is it evolution or invasion? He strokes my hand, feeling my skin
vibrate with every idea I remember. Dorothy, I simply
pointed out the machine at the center of the aliens' sub-
liminal labyrinth. That's why I'm their prisoner, a nybbuk,
wandering blind and forgetful down multiple poison al-

leys, mind in barbar borbor tatters.

◦ ◦ ◦

It's possible that evidence of the invasion is encoded in language. Kalium is the Latin word. And if, as I suspect, the Kalian aliens are a potassium-based life form, then a word like *tartar* might be of some significance, a clue from some freer time compressed like the bones of trees into the medial oil of the present. Tartar, a potassium compound, has long been associated with *food* and *change*: it is used as a rising additive in baking, is added to eggs to make meringues, and forms on the sides of wine barrels as a by-product of fermentation.

The elemental metal antimony, a relative of arsenic, forms certain deadly compounds once prized among poisoners. Its tartaric taste is typically masked with mustard, for it is not the chain, it's the links that clues orbit.

Tartar is also an archaic term generically meaning *barbarian*, or *hellish stranger*, and specifically refers to the Mongol hordes of the early Adolescent Ages. Interestingly, the Mongols didn't have a written language until Kublai Khan, Genghis's gene poolboy, commissioned one in the late Tea Shaman Century. The story of the Mongol invasions is recorded by the *losers*, an inversion of the pat caveat issued by every historian worth her Ph.D. *We're neck infested, TV-watching robots if we let the aliens keep on this way.* Of course, the Chinese probably just wrote what the Mongols ordered them to, invasion of consciousness; the hexagram means keep your composure when the sword is at your brain.

Or so Denny explained to Dr. Sax. *Or wait*—A potassium-based life form cognitively invaded the human species in order to prepare us for dinner, and the history of all this is recorded by a loser—*me?*—criminally insane—*incarcerated?*—drugged, in a room with a TV blaring, burning for someone about whom I dare not think. Who

is Denny? Another voice in my head? The Hôpital St.
Dizier is in Dulce, New Mexico, I think, or maybe Pine
Gap, near Alice Springs, in Australia. I don't think they
let you have cats in prison, except maybe in Berkeley?
What am I dreading? I suspect he's a genuinely autonomous split personality, embodied and emoting like a beacon warding the rocks, and we can potentially cover much
more ground twogather than we ever could alone. It's not
really my cat. Marx was right about Hegel forgetting: History *does* repeat itself. As farce.

○ ○ ○

There was something I should have done many years
ago. At the time I may not have known, as it was not yet
the past, so I had no way of regretting. If women must
indeed weep. Yet, it seems the signs were already accumulating like entoptic patterns in the blind spots of my
vision. Stay? Leave? Acorn? Oak? There are em-
pathizations KOH may be telecasting from Hawai'i, or
perhaps she's with Armamentia Bila making music at
Greenpoint, or maybe in Oakland, helping to organize the
toxic clean up.

From Pine Gap to Hawai'i is many thousands of miles.
From Dulce to Oakland is many hundreds of miles. What
if she's in Oakland and I'm in Pine Gap? Wherever Rose
Mountain is. In this small room, with only the cat's eyes
for illumination and communion, anywhere away from
here lies across a Pacific Ocean of the soul. I'll need a
balloon...

Her long Celtic face, she was one of those rare individuals who could say something in such a way that people
would actually *see* what she intended, a telepath, a not
totally unknown talent, but plagued with depression she
was. Her butterfly crashed at fourteen when she was gang
raped, and she became ensnared, one wing broken, in a
kind of psychic bondage to that maze of moments, the

memory from which she would sometimes leap like a phoenix, into the spirit unencumbered by her beautiful but shadowy and mourning body. If ever I get anywhere, if ever I find myself in a sea of faces, I will not cease searching for hers.

∘ ∘ ∘

"How do you explain your claims of the disappearance of billions of people?" Dr. Sax has been trying to assay me, assistants hovering. Perhaps trying again—I have no way of knowing. Live or Mama Rex? She may think of me as a raucous pet, but I can see the silver bear she wears around her neck, an ancient talisman to ward off demons with a show of strength. I think she intends to recommend me to the space program, throw me out the scapegoat hatch.

Really, she's just my size; I could walk a crooked mile in her shoes.

"Whose picture is this?"

They want to hear a story, so I tell them one.

"The truth this time," but the more I give them, the more they dope me, call me an insane liar. They can't handle the truth. I give them names, I give them dates in the future, but they continue to live in a state of denial. I can't tell if their drugs are any good, which is why I keep trying to develop cancer, as I know the radiation and chemotherapy, if nothing else, will block the effects of the implants.

"Do you think we're all doomed, then?" Dr. Sax asked me one day out of the maroon.

"Certainly," I replied. "If not this generation or the next, then soon to follow. The irrevocable processes are already in motion. When humans are semi-sentient blobs vibrating at the right frequency for consumption, there will no longer be a need for implanting false memories."

At this juncture she informed me she intended to increase my dosage. I've been so hurt and angry I haven't spoken to her in weeks. Relatively speaking—the sun is black as night, and the moon does not lux me with her light. If light can ever. Here it is a false friend, grim and gray beneath a bright exterior. The cat has a command center the size of a walnut, though doubtless not as wrinkly. Brachiators could travel swiftly throughout the Mothership. This malathione grove is owned by Infinite Star Systems. I wander groping for a gate, searching to bring something to hand. Hope soars infernal.

○ ○ ○

Denny's eyes pop open and attempt to focus on one of Scry's rosy red buttons. Jesus, am I fucked up. She's got to watch it with the dosage. I may be dissolving into my component parts.

There are several instances of simultaneous occupation in the literature. I don't mean those fleeting glimpses of everyday empathy or déjà vu, but profoundly bifurcating into two or more autonomous and bewilderingly aware consciousnesses, each the holographic whole of the independent other, staring at one another across a great divide, only a telepathic catwalk connecting the Urim to the Thummim. I suspect this is keyed to the metabolism of potassium, but research in this area has been spurned by the established institutions.

Denny can't resist Scry's interpsychic suggestion, as he raises his beatiface to her petaled sheath. They couple holding perfect stillness, kicking time away like blankets and exchanging their lead for gold.

That was long ago, when we all first met. Or split up. Or it could be an implanted memory, to cover up the fact that everyone's disappeared up the sux. I can't prove anything, not locked down in here. The schizotemporal side effects are exhausting me. I long for sleep.

○ ○ ○

When I was seventeen I met a man, and we fell in love. His name was Michael Harkus and he came from Diamond Bar, just east of La Puente. If you're facing southeast. Or was. He was seventeen, too, and Persian. Or maybe Portuguese. He's the one who wasn't sure. He was a dream. When we were nineteen we consummated our affair, and lived together in a hotbed of redneck meanness.

He was the first. I was sure. For a while. After a few months, I split, my sexual identity tangling on my peers, not liking what was happening in the mirror as their fists flew through the air. I ran back to the desert with its life underground and lost time with Lydia for the next five years, rattlesnakes in my veins.

I wonder where you are. Ronnie beat me up one night in old woman Mecartea's kitchen because Lydia, riding a vicious horse, told him I was queer. *A skinny, twinkling star.* I flew back and slammed into the refrigerator, mouth bleeding, tasting potash, only freon escapes.

The other thing that happened is that the first of my two friends to shoot himself in the mouth ricocheted out. *Away into the sky so far.* I must have fogged the memory of Tony's suicide. Five years later, when I was rolling verses two by two in La Cholla, I went back to Yucca Valley to visit my brother Will, and we ran into an old girlfriend of mine and Tony's.

"How's Tony these days?" I asked Breezy, shotgun plum forgetting. Her mouth dropped open, and Will snapped, "He's dead, man," with that grim sort of embarrassment my brother had when I made a drug-addled fool of myself. I saw the lights dancing in the sky over the desert. Although it's comments like that that may keep me here. I wonder if I borrowed her clothes if anybody'd notice me walking out, it's all a bewilderment. Lost in the jungle with deforestation arms on. The cognitive bureaucracy is forwarding the wrong messages. Her office mate is confused, the calm of her temporal oil slick erupting with foaming bibles of alterity. No fraternizing allowed, although there is inevitably a certain amount of furtive bundling in the closet, and any self-respecting short-order cook can carry a steaming platter to table 69. Kalians gather in hordes on the purple ridges—but will they numbingly continue to sux us or will they start to bite?

As protection from the forces, the aloe cactus can be used as a heat shield during re-entry, now the desert is the beach, and look who won, sourmash peat truck. Get yer ass stolen, gods be blessed, and grunt into the thermometer, you've got urine tire spectrum on tide pool geography. Thus is thurssy bungs out kindling for a get-going in the gardens, where you wouldn't know what ducks laid eggs nought noggins knocked heads in drubken kundalini log tossin. *Wrap it up!* Keep your pilt down. Knot in one knilday, heavy, "Cheese seizures seem so long," one is heard to complain, slurring say. It's about all the dictum the magistrates can mutter. The lines wrap around the prisoner like dialogic around a devious promise. The Kalians wave burning sticks of mind-wiping incense as they ride through the city. *Nothing's wrong*, they say, and all the humans on the block disappear up the sux. *No one here can help you.*

Only play-talk, the lost form of knowledge, can express what is otherwise unspeakable. It alone is free of disguise and ambiguity. A life of profound avoidance begins with not taking the first breath. It's possible I have things backwards, dyslexic autism, a lunar hexplanation. There is no knowledge without rhythm. The aliens have no vowels; their speech rattles around like bees on the psi-band. The secret task of philosophy may be the rediscovery of play. If allowed to interact uncoerced, spoken language arises spontaneously in groups of two or more children. That's the test, but what are the passwords?

Green anarchies of plant and meat echo pelagically, *everything is amniotic, everything is nothing.* There was something I was thinking the other minute; I can feel the reverberations. Trick of the light? I shake my head, and shyly smile at the particle traces. I leave, tracking uncertainly, the square root of two or seven and other delicacies. A piper pieds up, other pipers pan in—*I was fluting with you.* Cacophony is a kind of conversation at the physical level. *You hear me, then?* There's that old musical saw you in half again: Are the emanations of a thing dependent upon someone perceiving them? If a tree grows in Brooklyn, in other words, but everyone in Brooklyn has disappeared up the sux, does said tree not make a slow squeaking sound as it sprouts from the nut and pushes up through a crack in the pavement?

∘ ∘ ∘

I did not believe this in the bathtub where galaxies collide, shooting up in the private gallery of my grandmother Slackercode's bathroom. Soaking naked, fucking the arm with a needle, and we were all together, horses penned, and a synthetic orpheum, *fut*, my vein is dead, *bang*, my brain is full of sedimenting experience, *pine of bee stings.* Suddenly the implant wasn't such a big deal.

When I was with Tony Cross the UFOs were real, out on the desert on acid, then again with the slap in Santa Barbara. Borbor me timbers, there's that beautiful stranger from the Central Asian labyrinth wanting to get to know me better. *Again we dance*, is it only the wind making the stars sway? Tony is always present. I hear his voice; there is no mistaking his elven call. And there are weirder things, like letters from John of the Apocalypse, as if coincidence were synchronized to fall like rain somewhere far off soft, keeping the company of recusants.

We started to make a movie of the UFOs with our eyes, trekking miles across the Mojave, spotters wrecked. We found a brain that couldn't stop consuming, a trickster reflection. We had to be careful of the cholla, the jumping cactus puffballs of barbs, and the low-flying silent dark triangles on training missions out of Tartary.

∘ ∘ ∘

I remember the last time she ever touched me, knuckles such as she has brewen, hard-hewn in a pub where I had a dream. I was sitting for dazed, a statue of lapsis lazuli, and KOH, just back from her trip around the world, was unwilling to talk about the flight out of Bali, one wing broken. She thought I was from the future. *That could still be true for us?* As we parted, she touched my cheek with the tips of her fingers and clicked closed the door of her apartment.

Her eyes. I just want to see her eyes again, to feel the full flowering of our connection, windows onto the soul. Brown, tears pooling, spilling, as the words I can't remember tumbled out of my mouth, but my voice low, calm, perhaps beseeching her to understand the incomprehensible. *Why are you leaving me?* They are calling me with syringes of varying size. *Is that the river rushing through you?* I tie myself to the mast. I seem to recall we have two of the most common names in the phone book of the Western World, but maybe everything I know ricochets in an aquarium.

∘ ∘ ∘

I can see it in their pixilated faces. Like an enthymeme's missing premise, a gene is deleted, and the personal responsibility to remember loses force and spreads like an anesthetizing gas. The conspiracy blooms malignant, and they come in with the implants. The cities break open, boiling with pus. I don't know what it is anymore. *Mama said there'd be days.*

I've been dusting carefully, and operating at a thirty-third degree of detection-heightened awareness. "Did you hang large media ochre banners on your porch? Did you impotize any important words?" Interrogate the mortal. Dr. Sax has a new theory of Dianetics in her cupboard.

I have been analyzing terrorism for years. Rivers and gutters in lines of words, white-space gulches in paragraphs of riders. Terror is advertising, always making the alphabits big and tall or big and fat, letters that squeeze their graphemic cleavage. Gliders in the night out of nowhere smack my face, calling the slap magnanimous, but I know it's just inexorable. Propaganda straps to my brain like leather, like a belt; they figure my holes will become larger just where the tolerance is stretching.

We are the mortal humans, rushing with bloods full of hallucinations and growth. The belligerent aliens will be repelled—a motto adopted because it gives hope to the damned. Immunity is a lottery ticket. Addiction is an exhausting fascination. Memory is an allotment check drawn on a Kalian bank. The world is a tough audience, *days like this.*

○ ○ ○

I was once slapped by an invisible force. The slap woke me up, so it's possible I didn't see the slapper. But I believe I wasn't deeply asleep, that I woke up quickly, that I searched the area with swift and silent thoroughness. The most rational thing I can think of is that the slap was from a bird's wing, an owl perhaps. But this didn't feel like feathers, or a hand. More like hot plastic, just below the ignition point. It was an enlightenment of fear, a blow from the invisible master I didn't think I had.

○ ○ ○

Everything cults, cuts, on the krauts of others. I'm bifurcating, searching for a word, but the line is busy. *Evia cotta abruia.* Lambasting the jabberwocky, the Metaphor Police sirened into the Victorian Dive and busted all the windows in my apartment. But I cannot answer the aliens' questions; I cannot begin to face them, I am less than, the question I have is: When will I face *them?* Lydia glares at me from under the bed. I am in touch with *them* as much as my mediations and questions form such contact; this is *here* where it is. Whenever I can tell you I will, but what the name forgets might never be recalled.

Everything is different from up here, I hear her breathing. I can't think straight, I can't act straight. I've got to act like a goat, some kind of animal is possessing me, I have the ruts, the come-get-me, the suck-slut-happy rump-up all-is-forgiven fuck-me blues. Like a paranormal earthquake to a faultless ley line. *I had to go*, remembered the ancient astronomer with grim remorse. That was when we heard them, *We'll have to explode their heads*. Like relatives, we emigrated to Madagascar, which we perceived as slowing and moving away from the soulless city into the unknown clouds of the spiritual world. Too slowly, apparently, for the tart tastes of some, who call us sloths and lorises, lemurs of our former selves.

o o o

Up against the wall of hell o'vision, and speaking a strange and barbaric tongue, I would still be your lover. *I saw you in the mirror*. The aliens have a thousand damned eyes. We are caught in the tides of history, paying for security with a permanent state of anxiety. We humans respond with toadying, maneuvering, and ventriloquism in anticipating the whims of the implants, which inspire more inner trembling than the old enemy. *You were looking over my shoulder*.

I took it from KOH, incredulous. I felt as if my eyes were glued to the vid screen. With her, I understood perfectly how space might be curved. *Every pixel a pore*. We require an education in media as in the sentiments in order to discover that what we assumed—with the complicity of our teachers—was culture is in fact nature, that what was given is no more than a way of taking. And we must learn, when we take, the cost of our participations, or else we shall pay much more. We shall pay our capacity to love at all. *Pouring over every bit of information, looking for the pattern.* A reflection of this is discernible between individuals. Anyone who is categorized in advance as implanted—without having signed the imaginary declaration that seems to unite the true believers, who recognize each other by something imponderable in gesture and language, as by a pass phrase—will repeatedly have the same experience. *The pattern of your face.*

∘ ∘ ∘

I saw them walking, singing a round, or perhaps drinking, friends must stay together. Rockets flew in space, and cosmonauts sat in them. We even had their pictures on our matchbooks—and the aliens tasted us like bread. Doctors, I begged, help her—try to rouse her again. She has shot herself into my brain. *Eyes before ease, and each to her season.*

It was the right year, measured in TV space-time, the Year of the Lipid Receptor Protein, viral municipalization, nuketide in Soma, the Lesbian capture of the Bridge, and for a few dollars more you can get an implant on the Mothership, courtesy of PanAmnesic Airlines. *Neighbors away.* Because I was in jail, then as now. Or was I, by Bell's Theorem, supraliminally connected to what in fact turned out to be part of my future's history? *Friends, friends to the end...*

I don't remember the loneliness of those times. Women must weep. Tony rang that day from Gorda, the outer level, to say he was going to begin his ascent to the upper regions of the lowest depths of Kalian Hell. I couldn't remember the country code for Tartary—would he be able to find a zone? It may have been around the same time that I slipped on a crack and broke my mother's back. *A shot heard 'round the world.* I think I got pulled up the sux, but was returned to find the pillow key. On Earth, or my body, blind, deaf, and dumb, wishing I could know for sure, verdant sward greenly gladed. All I remember are sounds. First, rushing wind, like something lifting at incredible speed. Then the hollow harmonics in long frequencies that can only come from an immense, enclosed space. Last, a lark calling arpeggios and a breeze like the sound of a feather whispering from across the cell.

○ ○ ○

Years before, Tony told me and Jim Hayes and Michael Harkus that the aliens were a slogan-manufacturing company that had tried to take over his father's Coors distributorship. Jim, whose father was a golf pro, nodded knowingly. Michael, whose father was probably a vagabond doper with long hair and tats, though nothing was known for sure, stared at Tony as if trying to triple-guess him. My own father, I realize now, tried, as so many have, to escape the aliens through alcohol. At the time, though, I had no idea what Tony was talking about so I burst out laughing and then we were all laughing because we were really high on black triangles and sitting in the middle of the desert with nobody but the owls and coyotes to give us any monitor gain.

Twenty years later, hiking with Armamentia Bila up to Mitchell Caverns, in the Providence Mountains, way the hell out in the desert between Car Stole and Lost Wages, I looked over my shoulder and saw a matte-black stealth fighter jet. We didn't hear it, and only saw it for a few seconds before it disappeared behind a craggy tangent. Twenty-seven years earlier, I had gone to the caverns with my Girl Scout troop. I qualified as a member on a technicality, and don't recall us seeing any back-engineered black triangles flitting around.

○ ○ ○

Armamentia Bila was my wife. *Daimon?*

Bila posited the *sphota*, which is something other than a discontinuity, though all the while being revealed by the discontinuous. If these words, heaped upon me by angels and aliens, can be abstracted by analysis and exist as real entities in a sentence, and letters similarly exist in words, then letters should themselves be capable of division, just as atoms are. With the right prescription. Since the identification of self-sufficient parts is not possible in a letter, there should be neither the letter nor, as a consequence, the word. And when neither letter nor word can be established, how can meaning be conveyed? *The demon Strable splits the heart in two with his arrow of triangulation.*

The doctors always ask me, at some point, "And who was Bila to you?" Just the last name, as if saying both together could cast a spell.

"My wife," I answer.

"Yes, but what did she *mean* to you? What did you *do* together?"

To keep my sanity I have to assume such questions are rhetorical. The answers are indigestible. To assuage their grief, the men share the body of their dead lover as a meal. They build a fire by a spring and fill the time by sharing goddess stories, conspiracy theories, speaking their utopian dream of a universal cunnilingus.

But what is to be done if the direct and sole vocation of every intelligent man is babble, that is, the intentional pouring of water through a sieve? A war arose between Chronos and Titan. The gods introduced a diversity of tongues. We built the demon's tower, in ruins now, its name lost in the confusion.

◦ ◦ ◦

Naked in a cell, nothing to do but go insane. I once taught arrhythmitic, simultaneous calculus, and manicmatics at the local high school. I may have been molesting students; there appears to have been some fairly damning evidence published in the local paper. *The only one?* When the guards shaved me they deliberately nicked me, then berated me for smearing blood all over the virus-gray walls. Actually, I just explained why and how to use a condom, which somehow became a demonstration of how to override the implants. *Radiation therapy.* Oneirica's sexiness brings on wars. There is no faking it with the aliens around. *I wasn't messing around.* That gangster Margarine'll poke your eyes out in a room filled with cigarette smoke. *You're the one who inhaled.* The one thing we in prison want is some peace and quiet to meditate upon our sins, but there is none of that. *You're cesium up.* The TVs blare all day; the real loonies howl and chatter and rant. Some of the rants are deeply compelling, like the stare of an owl or a cat, heartbeat cascades of passionate renderings. *Like the night you oiled us together and then rolled us apart.* You either eat or get the tube. Maybe a lobotomy, if you're lucky. It's nothing like an afternoon of baseball, hotdogs, and beer.

A medical segregation, they call it. "Just say human," hisses the snake, chromosomes chain-link cycling in a biological narrative. I'm just a reporter, Red Sea parted, a recorder—if not an angel, then a cipher fashioned of blood and spume in the likeness of Aquaknowledge. Divining Metatron shrugs his cyrillic shoulders, and clears a golem from his throat.

○ ○ ○

I rose up that morning, thinking of hitting the lab, waking up with the sick panicked knowledge that something must be done. I'd had an eldritch dream, which would occur again and again many times over the years with vicious and explicit variations, the background notion radiating sex and death, the coated lips that polish the head of culture. *Ignore the gravity.* I can vaguely remember sounds, voices from the dream, immense perspectives, presences, a darkness that welled like a high-desert night sky. I was standing before a huge, squeaking city gate, turning through my backpack, desperately hoping to find a rosary in the burning bush. Or maybe a phone number. Or a cigarette. I could hear murmurings about memory fatigue syndrome coming from the professional lounge, and spent a long time arguing with Will about death as the end of remembering. Or maybe it was just dark. But by the time I woke up I had to have some potassium. *No rules for Mercury.*

Hitch the Luther-fucking hike out of here, like only frug-easy motels will give me booking in the disintegrating dawn of raw-thumbed paradise and injunction, KOH is out there somewhere. I must discover— Dreams are images, like hexagrams or liberating rockets, not interpretations—am I drifting, I—

The cat bats a dust cunny like a topplegänger and her double comes out to play. *You can't tell them apart.* Lydia came over to the cabin one hot afternoon, took off her shirt and smiled. Nairbula smiled back because he wasn't yet afraid. I was still in astronomy school. Red hair swaying, like someone signaling from a rocky swerve of shore. I lay down with her and touched her breasts, pressed my lips to hers, my hand returning home to succor. Love's long later I learned that her kitten play was her revenge on Flika Oswald, a revenge that exploded like magnesium in Nairbula's light-sensitive eyes.

I wonder if the cat remembers anything outside this cell. Nairbula had no resistors, and who could resist the gravitational pull of Lydia's stellium in Leo? I am the pilot of my own perturbation. Though I still can feel the timbre of things, my own memories, after so long, are losing saturation, ergot my metal urgency.

○ ○ ○

The recovery of memories from heliotropic vats requires strategies beyond speech. *Light-years of hearing.* I need hologrammatic communication—telepathy—in order to confront the aliens. I need instant, verifiable, shared data—physical contact—in order to determine the exact vector of the epidemic. *Images of heaven.* The color green continues to appear to me in circumstances bound to attract my attention, messages that I interpret as a summons from Rose Mountain. The trip may not be easy, but even if for only a moment of memory it may be worth the effort. I need KOH. I thought there was already a word for this? *Cauldron.*

The narratological universe is supraliminal, allows for paranormality. I may have drifted for a moment, I was— *There's been significant progress in brain chemistry since you were a student, Professor Nairbula. Perhaps you should let me try.* I am suspicious of Dr. Sax's offer. I tell her I'm not a joiner, that I don't care about passing for human. A private place in the mountain sphere, my medulla's been through enough. They can't jack into what they can't pin down. *And the Dogons keep rolling along.* I scratch the back of my neck, remembering.

Are we such soft-brained implantees that we consider this cruel technology simply another environmental constraint to be ignored, like gravity or breathing? Our history has been completely overrun by the ultimate winners, the tartaric aliens who need not even be physically present to corral and milk us for our psychic juices, which they slurp like soup in their orbiting cupboards.

◦ ◦ ◦

I bash up through the surface, gasping, splashing, trying to remember my true name. I was trapped in a tunnel, perhaps a mine, or the hall of some valley lord. For your lips will still be warm with her lips, I remember Armamentia told me one rainy day in April. For your hips will still be aching with the gravity of her embrace. She must have meant KOH. *My secret garden.* If she happens to resemble one or several women in your dreaming life, you will continue to search for her through your waking hours. Sailors set out on perilous journeys just so they can see in actuality cities they have only imagined. I remember something I should have done, should have done a long time ago.

∘ ∘ ∘

The aposiopetic individual presents with tics, convulsions, repetitive speech with linguistical dementia, and a silk-pink glow around the entire body. As opposed to the ghosts commanded by the demon Strable, *split infinitive*, the aliens are internal spirits, spirits who may possess people by entering their heads and controlling their speech and movements. Beware the jury of our peers that is the judge of our assassins—be not deceived by appearances. References. *Necks.* St. Anthony's fire descends like sulfuric acid boiling through the skin.

The woman who taught me this was Michael Harkus's mother, I seem to think her name was Eris. She coupled one nocturne with a handsome fly-by-night sailor porchgull Iberian (technically a suave and earthy Moor) and conceived Michael. Call her Eris. This was way before I met Armamentia or Lydia and things broke down into begging food from haughty lemurs for our hungry veins. Tony and I used to hitchhike out there all the time.

We used to take acid and clean her house. Eris's house was a cabin out on the desert which took half a day to hitch and hike to, but we couldn't get there short of three-days' hike if we had to all the way. Out on the Mojave northwest of the capital of Dreamland, Twentynine Palms, Eris's cabin was chucked down behind a clutch of bluffs that acted like a censor to the wind. Which howled, and gave everything a battened-down look. I guess it was more than just a look. It's true, east along the branch of Highway 62 off the arterial I-10, they talked about "wind, death and taxes." Potassium was not the first word out of Chris Cross's mouth—Chris, who called himself Tony, later pistol shot myself through the upper palate into his brain, born by cesium section.

Away the lysergic anchor, set the sail, push out into the desert, follow the prophet of the day deep into the trailing night. Bad boy but kind, Tony the Trickster, a coyote among robots, laughing in the face of losing his mind from chasing injected memories, quick-quipping for his life. He trapped miles below his soles heading forth the drummers in the Trojan marching band and driving a tattoo into the skin of the street beneath the parade route. His snare was vigorous and his breath was deep. Inside, it was cool and dim, but it got dusty fast; the wind didn't just blow; it rattled the dust in. The world is an osmotic pressure cooker. We cleaned a lot.

He always failed with women, and eventually shot himself. Somehow, none of this happened the way I remember; everything in place splits apart. The pedestal can't center the statue. He couldn't deal with consensus reality, which put him on the wrong side of the scientists we met one moonless night, who wanted to consume us like we watch TV. The implant drove Tony insane; it was the thing that crossed him up. I am the last believer, maybe, of his old friends. The others—Michael Harkus, Jim Hayes— have disappeared in the dust clouds on the horizons of life. Or worse. I wish I had been the trigger; I wish I had been the bullet.

No, I don't want to be the weapon in a murder. I'm going crazy in here. I love the man passionately but I cannot become his death, as much as I want to bring him back. You don't walk barefoot through the desert. I hate the rocket-fuel taste of regret, hiding behind the moon.

Mouth in the secret mirror, knee at the pillar of pride, hand with the bar of a cage: proffer yourselves the dark, spiel my name, lead me to him. *Me*. Tony's suicide is proof that there are glitches in the alien broadcast gestalt, that their control over us is not total, that we are still the vital pigmies singing *who* in the thick of things.

∘ ∘ ∘

I was hitchhiking, and landed in Santa Barbara for the night. Tony was dead, but I didn't know that yet. My old high school had fences around it by then, to screen out mad potassium bombers and drug dealers, to chicken coop truants in a box of pessimism padded with false promises. I walked down the people's street toward the giant old meeting-place tree that was destroyed by fear and politics a few years later, as illuminated by Garry Trudeau many years ago. I had stood at the foot of Gorda all day, the fat old-woman spirit hill that blocks the way back north to Big Sur. Or she did, at least, until the NORAD Corps of Ingénues came through long ago and installed rocket launchers on that particular bend of bay. But, of course, that wouldn't happen for some time to come, and as it was already dark, I crawled under a wide hedge in a side-street front garden, and rolled out my sleeping bag. Quiet as a mutant, so as to avoid attracting any unneighborly attention.

I could see a TV-blue window from my green hide out, but felt certain I was completely concealed from the lamp-lit street and nearby homes. I lay back and positioned myself so that I could look up at the black sky through the bushes. I remember falling towards sleep quickly. It had been a hard day, a driver had tried to shake me down for sex; I had to jump out of his car in a lonely place where no cars came, and ended up standing on a freeway on-ramp for hours beneath the instigating sun rotating orange 'round Gorda.

I had barely dropped off when abruptly I was slapped, sharply, stingingly. I jolted upright, whirling around, looking for my assailant. No one there. Nothing moved. I heard nothing, not a sound. I glared into the moonlit shrubs and out across the lawn, but nothing stirred. I stared and stared, scared out of my wits—the slap *hurt*, *something* hit me *hard*—but damn it nothing appeared, moved, no one came forward to explain this smiting.

To this day it remains a complete mystery to me, one that comes floating out like ephemera from the pages of a difficult book. Every explanatory theory I have seems utterly ridiculous. An owl's wing? Tony's ghost in the bush? A neural glitch? An alien invasion? I silently leaked tears from loneliness, fear, the vastness of the sky, and the shivering of vertigo as I careered into the void. Eventually I fell asleep again.

◦ ◦ ◦

I forgot to escape and left her idling in the rail station, getaway all planned. The trance comes from the base of the spine and the center of the neck, the reptilian brain concerting out through the ganglia to couple with the dragon, following the kundalini mainline tracks. My lover, KOH, can sing the names of our hearts' desires; she leads with her breasts and I follow her hips and pulse the rhythms to this song, all that she taught me, like every mammal's heart that beats, this is what comes sedimenting down to us, I am a slobbering human, only wanting this planet. We are rooted in a swamp, and our branches twine and graft each twogather; gasping out of water we speciate with fractal delicacy, and there is no balance, only the chatter and calling of true names, for we are rank with mud.

It might just be adrenaline. *"The damage to her right brain has in effect blinded her to consensus reality, a kind of emotional amnesia which presents linguistically."* I have to get out of this bin and find KOH. My level of awareness of monitoring is rising.

∘ ∘ ∘

Tony, just before the end, told me his telepathic link with the aliens had opened the door to the cognitive invasion. This was a little after I stole his girlfriend, Breezy. It couldn't be helped—Breezy and I were irrepressible together, my Christian Brothers brandy and guitar, and her long-winged songbird voice. How could something so real be false, a forged memory inserted into my brain under phony proscenia?

I think Tony was wrong that night at Breezy's. We drank a ridiculous amount of beer. He showed up, unannounced, bearing a case of Coors, like old times. Peace party, an intoxicated offering to the quixotic goddesses of love. Tony never actually said why he came over that night. When Breezy and I played our song, "We Dare the Aliens to Land," he got weird. Panicky. He gesticulated wildly. His voice oscillating into its upper octave, he kissed the words out of his mouth as if they were precious and he was going to miss them terribly after they flew through his lips. But he talked rapidly, careening, as if an emergency mission had taken him into an ancient Babylonian hall of mirrors.

It wasn't Tony's being telepathic, in particular, that opened the door to the invasion. The terrains of consciousness, speech, and telepathy all have common borders. Telepathy is a terrifying forest we're rightly fearful to enter. But it may be that the darkling forest, once crossed, meadows in the lap of Rose Mountain, where the aliens can't come.

I once knew a woman with an expansive telepathic sense. The aliens forced me to part ways with her; long-range forecasts predicted we'd be dangerous together. A rubber-gloved surgeon with huge snake eyes extracted the organ, but missed all the areas of holographic redundancy. Perhaps that's why the transpiration of our brief love affair has come to burn so brightly over time, KOH having intuitively, interpsychically, grasped so much more than I could have ever said. *Or not said.*

I must find her. Which is a bit like a person submerged naked in water saying, "I will now inhale." I think I've been here for seventeen years, incommunicado, with no prospect for a change of circumstances. I must break the glass, let water run where it may.

My theory is that the aliens have been sucking on our dreams for tens of millennia. They've got a huge bureaucracy going, Earth's invisible government, covered with blind scabs and riddled with gorged organs, and I feel as lucid as I have in years. *If you could only remember my name?* Can they have forgotten about me?

○ ○ ○

Does she think of me? When things go wrong? When things go right? Our telepathic link must make me present to her in some nameless way, possessing her with a reflective pause from time to time. And she must be reaching out for me with her mind, which is why I miss her more than the sun. Or even music. She listens to music; I can almost hear it sometimes, it pulses through my nerves, waves of music. She spends a great deal of time seeking out beautiful music, music that bathes her in emotional color, colors to relieve the chronic gray of her heart, which is blue. *Quiet, here they come.*

I never know if any of this is true; there are no reference points. I can neither hear, see, nor speak either truth or evil, discounting the TV, which I must as it can't be trusted. Can't be turned off. It could be that I'll die soon. Seventeen years? But was I thirty or forty when this began? Presumably, then, I could be as much as fifty-seven years old. Expectancy-wise, that might be a little young.

To die. Not to escape. To what, I have no idea. An even darker corner, perhaps, the things I see on TV now surrounding me, porous moderns, a shallow, slow-moving swirl of cess, impossible to suss.

There is no point in killing myself with regret quite yet though. I have a bootstrap to ascend. Bifurcate me, pleat me, humus the underwritten. We b'weave the world is entwined, a fragment of a fractal, a curve equation, the verb *to be. An image of the future.* Stolen by aliens. Calling out to the guard in front of me, trying to get off the train, lux Lucifer plucked free by the damned chance, playing Strable. I don't think he recognizes my face, coming unto the narrative like narcotics to a free market. *They can give you a medicated bath for this, you'll feel much better.* I can't tell us apart.

The reed harp was left in the wind to play, a signal to whoever might happen by. Leave things in the rafters, good rot comes from random fermentation, go hang it, age your head like a sausage, go like the wild yeast and invent the brew. Frig the Nazi combustion logic creep humpen in teas of nouveau neurotics, clueless and Bible-pounding Astral-fucking-goths. All cattle kept looping isotopes long-chained during Apollo's reign on the grassy knoll. We clowned hermetically, frowning like fanatics or people famously upset. I stole his cattle; it had got into their milk.

The cat stirs, licks her paw. I think she imagines specks of dust. Nothing moves in here. Still, re-infection is always a threat, so I can understand her caution. The aliens killed Tony, after all.

○ ○ ○

I strike Olympia from behind, hard, in the back of the skull. I catch her as she falls. *Gently now.* Her shoes are a difficult fit. They don't recognize my feet, but they'll have to do. I don't forget to steal her keys. I run with the cat in my arms through the hallways in Dr. Sax's skirt, bra and

blouse, my legs about to pop out of her nylon stockings. I
can't find an exit sign, and it bites me that this must be a
prison hospital, lines on the floor leading ever deeper inside. I try the keys on locked doors, but find only more
hallways. I hadn't counted on a labyrinth—I psigh into
soul space, trying to suss the leys. Then I just move, because nothing matters if I'm standing still. The cat jumps
from my arms and sprints down a corridor, and I run to
catch her. We dash through a dayroom with blaring TVs
watched by drool and mirror-glass eyes. Through a window in a revolving door across the room I see another
window far down a hall, and it's unmistakably leaking
sunlight. I scoop up the cat and run like hell.

Lost Blue Marble

IT'S WORSE THAN I THOUGHT.

If I just keep talking they won't be able to hear me think. The party of the third part, begin, the self-same egalitarian standing probe, I hear but will not pay, implant yawning in the neck. Party of the second part, begin. They do not know me, this topic has not yet arrived, they are the terrorists who will come to flame me where I stand. Everything is on all the time out here, too, unsuspecting party of the first part.

Begin. A door revolves, unhinged melody, the pillow key in plain sight, a wounding ruse, a poignant reminder of the techniques they use to nebulate our kuru-ridden minds. The cat huddles in my arms, ghost rider. Assume nothing but the position. What if somebody asks me her name?

It's eerie out here; I'm not quite myself. *Just follow the shadow on the anima moondial.* My voice takes on various disguises, no effort on my part. Do I speak—or is it perhaps someone else who is talking, and I forget, and think it's me? This is not unheard of among enthymemics, a cerebral cascade of passports counterfeited in some crummy backroom, a skip-tracer's nightmare, ill-lit and infested with assumptions. I need to keep talking when words fail me for fear of the silence that lies at the heart of the end.

○ ○ ○

Is this Australia or New Mexico? More importantly, which way to KOH? Left or south? Historians are gathering on the horizon. Questions are posed like pudenda coupling with other members of the tribe; meaning is fecund. The unbearable solicitude of the media, burning from every orifice, heaving every corner, glaring in the wash of its scalding rays. Temporales, über alles. *Go forth and multiply.* I spray paint a negative of my eagle-spread hand on the brick wall like a sign in the labyrinth.

∘ ∘ ∘

My convulsive ticcing gives the cat a pretty rough ride, but I have to keep moving. She clings to my shoulders, often hiding beneath my hair, especially when the static becomes excruciating. Sometimes she hunts mice, though she's frequently disappointed, as what she's caught is really a wandering projection device. I myself never had a RAM disk; I wasn't in with that crowd, and don't regret it. Any stimulated electron can be used as a carrier wave to bear the aliens' incessant messages of falseness, betrayal, and doom. And for what, a snack?

Some cats possess a rank odor, but fortunately this one doesn't. It's the smelling salts. Though I don't remember her as being gray. Requis, cat. Which is odd, because I did once have a gray cat. Mouche, her name was, which means *fly* in French and *mouse* in Persian. Mouche was more French—snobby, saucey—although she did little dervish dances when she whirled at flies, whence her name. I never would have known to name her that, Armamentia named the bedraggled kitten. *Come in out of the cold and rain, out of trapped Tyre.*

Under such conditions, I can't help wanting to be free. The cat locks onto my eyes with her telepathic light; she reflects an image into my mind. She gazes in the direction of the future. She has caught scent of KOH.

I feel feverish. It could be my body fighting the dystemporalexia. Or the curried ketamine. Mustn't stare at the sky. Mustn't be fearful of what circles above, omens pointing laser-beam fingers, they'll fry my sun-spotted ass.

Keep it slathered with aloe gel, there's a good— *What?*

I'm taking my life in my hands because of the wheat circles separating from the chaff. It feels like a highly localized vibration progressing up my spine, spreading a tingling from my buttocks up to the top of my skull. The aliens sux the accumulated memories and emotions of the day, but they're sloppy. They leave fragments and sometimes whole whorls, but then again, I always find myself someone else.

∘ ∘ ∘

I'm not a lesbian. I just look like one. We never lived together, so it wasn't the software. We all got separated, perturbated by the orbiting sux. Love was not for me while winter lasted. Our world was flying apart, like so many birds taking wing in different directions. Collisions were inevitable. "Far from being a perverted monster, she is the logical and inescapable product of her culture, with its secrecy and restrictions," the Borbors said, or maybe the bourboned guardians, but aren't they all just voices from outer space, chasing my tail? Logos Khan job, the demon Strable is a blinding light. Into the thought that was like a brazen stone I flung the dead dog; out of the thought that was like a bower I plucked roses and jasmine.

Dr. Sax on the phone—*"Astrocytosis, presenting with profound mnemosine hallucinatory states, and uncinate seizures."* "Can you hear me Scry? *Scry?*" Prosopagnosia? "Is that you?" Denny doesn't seem to recognize her face. *"Enthymemic aposiopesis, compounded with severe linguistic diaspora"*—clamoring from the concentration camp.

The noiseless din that I have long known in dreams booms at me in waking hours from television walls. I am driven to do this, to do that, against my will. No doubt in the Adolescent Ages this was literally seen as possession. Danny Kaye appears to have had a convulsive tic, but this may have been acting. In psychoanalysis nothing is true but the exaggerations. He's dead now, or so they'd have us believe. The Red King on the Mothership dreams of me. *Spread your loving arms way out in space.* We can tell if we're happy by the sound of the wind, *when May comes to make the hedges green with its green veil over every lovely greenwood.*

Lugubrious vats of ectoplasmic foam in stationary orbit behind the moon. Unfortunately, dark-side images over-amp all, and the contrast of all imagining is blown out by the blue noise from the TV tanks telling us what to remember. *To feed the fish.* I keep trying to *see* solutions to problems, rather than uncarving my block and making myself like a wind sock. One mighty wing-spread blast of combined psychic energy—a rebel yell—might stun the aliens for long enough to allow us to wake up and regroup on the village green. This is because Styx Valley is depicted as a primeval world, a place of origin, the place where several of the mythical invaders land and which becomes the gathering place for the dead. Somewhere far off a shaman transforms the abandoned pulp mill into a butterfly, softly fluttering towards Hawai'i.

To convulse is to leap over several moments. *You lose time*, is what we say. *Blackout.* But what we may be witnessing is temporary temporal agnosia, the fissile matter of memory-scattering particles in alpha wave-shearing blasts as the megawatt epileptic bomb from deep within the brain explodes to the surface, *fryen all day tender young asses.* This was reported to me by A.A. McDruthers. We were sitting in his North Beach squat drinking cheap red lightning, the shopping cart providing a modicum of privacy, down to our last forty-thousand cigarettes since I don't remember when.

Lesbian is such a weird word. I wonder if Clodia ever felt like this. Before we parted ways, Dr. Sax provisionally agreed to receive my thermal report. An advance from savagery to barbarism, I warned her that what she hears on TV is just the gurgling of aliens, the lies of bottom-feeding plagiarists. Lesbos is a treasured island, an idea, a place of reproduction, of stories, its illuminators Sappho and Catullus, the gay poets of green summer, rosy-cheeked in a mountain forest. I think that fact has finally hit home, and so nothing seems to get lost, repressed, in the process. Or so the doctors tried to tell me, *money-back guarentee*, and when they did I knew they couldn't be trusted, or were perhaps simply utterly unreliable, as things have only gotten worse since the invention of agriculture. *Invasion of aliens.* I expect she'll want to tommy-knock me when she wakes up. In the reel time, every image I see on TV makes me feel fat. Ugly. I lean against a store window and vomit. My desire minotaurs against me. *Tear down the pin-ups.* The cat leaps from my shoulders and pads down the street. Anyway we say it, the pass phrase is: *barbar tartar borbor.*

∘ ∘ ∘

Denny stares into the yolk running magma in the bowl of my Special K.

∘ ∘ ∘

Who stared too long at the gulag? Who gazed into the burning intoxication of the wall? Who gnawed on the bars of steel? Who tried to slobber-acid dissolve the concrete base? Whose finger tore knotting itself in the keyhole?

The moon is a pulse in the fundament. The Rosenbergs will fry under the desert sun, outcasts from the hollow interior of the Earth, strapped to chairs in Times Square at high noon. *"How many nuclear reactors were there and what sorts of accidents?"* Just before disappearing up the sux, people on the east coast of Oneirica experienced a sudden rise in K levels; it must have been syzygy. The Harmonians first exploded a loRad in the Year of Aye Carumba. After that, it became a fashion.

The only rule is: Don't let history repeat itself. That statement may be a farce. I tighten down the hatches on the sides of my skull. Tiny pipes that snip create a measured, germinal way.

The insurgents demand a system restart. They nuke the western span descending from Treasure Island into Cern Francisco, somatosis. People are nervous; the I/O becomes boggy with back-up, thrashing heap and stack, flimsy boats in the wake of a beater clipper ship orbiting in the mouth of the tossing bay.

What difference is this all, after prophets profligate answers like swerving turns, all this difference is—*traffic!* What is this? I stumble though intersections waiting for lights to change, as if their blinking eyes are gods. *What breaks, KOH, how I loved you, it is nothing now, again, you're gone, I am here, and every name has the taste of your name around it, bathed in salt water.*

○ ○ ○

"Give me to it!" I think I hear Denny yell, but how can that be? I feel a hit of bifurcation coming on.

"I"—Is the ego-iconic but still invertebrate Anglo-Saxon pronoun a hologram for ideotechnology? I, robot? *To toil bereft.* Yod is the finger that points, and the primates gibber and clutch themselves in fear, their faces lit like players in some ghostly drama of Ur.

You will visit all the stations of the Cross in a limousine, and be made glorious.

I'll explode their heads. Or pacify the lion fish. Or deacidify their ribonucleic solution. If I could just kiss the hem of Her garment, cherry blossom baptism. Aquaknowledge, winter me not in the springtime of our love.

○ ○ ○

Deep is the aching wound of this planet. KOH is praying to the goddess in a cathedral not made by hands. She once told me the universe had never been created. I can see her reflection in the cat's eyes. *This is all an illusion*, she said, which left me a little shaky, uninsured. I want to bend and kiss her neck, but refrain. *The aliens are listening*. It was just an idea. The rituals have protected us from the bombardment. They try to invade us with heavy, inert, and socially awkward cover-girl particles, ponderous iso-topes of argon which attack the sebaceous glands, releasors of the vitalizing, saliva-dancing chemical sebum, a niche of chemistry deeply involved with the pharmosemiosis of kissing, bonding, memory, and telepathy.

Christ the criminologist, am I walking in circles? Re-visiting the seam of the crime? I may have passed this beauty parlor an hour ago. I palm the shop window and spray paint another migrating bird. The Necks don't even look up as they stand on Zanzibar.

∘ ∘ ∘

"Argument is war. Metaphorical constructs structure everyday life. The essence of metaphor is understanding and experiencing one kind of thing in terms of another. The physical body is the heart of this notion, the over-flowing source of the Nile, consciousness its symptom."

I can't tell if the voice is coming from inside or outside. Could it be the guerrilla, Lakoff? Never sure, I creep around the corner and huddle with the cat in back of a dumpster. A Neck comes striding down the middle of the street, boot jax electronically perpetuating indulgences from above. I hope nothing bad happens.

"It is not that arguments are a subspecies of war. Argu-ments and wars are different kinds of things—and the actions performed are different kinds of actions. But ar-gument is partially structured, understood, performed, and talked about in terms of war—indefensible claims, attack-ing an argument's weak points, being right on target with critique, demolish a hypothesis, win a debate: if you've a different idea, shoot, you'll be wiped out if you use that strategy. They shot down all of my ideas." *Who is he talking to?*

"Imagine a culture where argument is viewed as a dance, the participants are seen as performers, and the goal is to perform in an ecstatic and aesthetically pleasing way. In such a culture, people would view arguments differently, experience them differently, carry them out differently, and talk about them differently. But *we* would probably not view them as arguing at all: they would simply be doing something different."

○ ○ ○

I saw Scry kissing Denny a long time ago near the Golden Goat Bridge, but how can that be? I never knew anyone before I knew KOH and she was the last person I knew before I was hospitalized. Incarcerated? *Escaped.* There is clearly something false in the above statement, like a ghost at a tea party where I can't see the leaves for the smoke—I don't actually remember ever being at such a party. But I turn the corner and there they are, kissing in the long shadows cast by the tall trees ringing the green. I was standing on the rough of the eighth hole, golf balls shooting like marbles through the glassy water, and I was wearing Denny's shoes and lips, so now I conclude that since the night he met Scry, Denny and I have simply split up in order to cover more ground.

There's a great deal to search for, but few ways of finding any of it. The only way to cure the ache of the old is with the new. Chance favors the well prepared mind; *disponibilité*, we make the road by walking. I think the cat is trying to tell me she needs to drink some water. The same could be said of me.

○ ○ ○

No one came after me. I even waited. The front of the prison hospital is a retail shop that sells buttons and things with which to sew them. I'm afraid of the word. On the way out I grabbed a kit and stuck it in my bra. Ideally, if fully prepared and on the safe side, I would bring the whole world with me. I must not fail. Perhaps I'll be able to trade the stitching tools for some cat food. And lemonade would be good. There was a TV in the shop. I stood staring at it for just a second, and when the cat said something, I suddenly realized that no one was following me. I shimmied out the front door in Dr. Sax's clothes and walked down the street.

I haven't seen a human the entire time I've been out. I'm not sure if this is significant. Bodies gawking around, but lacking the telepathic glow that marks most living things. Animated corpses? Samurai zombies? More likely, highly tweaked pseudanthropic Necks sent down from the Mothership to facilitate the suxing of the general population. Not even a dog. And, by my notch stick, I've been out here for sixteen days. Or hours, those could be.

It's all coming back to me: Styx Valley is in Colorado, and a helicopter will take too long. But there goes Margarine Not Butter!

"Butter," I mutter as loud as I can. The cat stares at me, surprised to hear human speech after so long, although this may be misrepresentation.

"*Not* Butter," she replies, and crosses the street my way, head cocked, looking to see who hailed.

I step out of the shadowed alley, my hand doing double duty in a sun-shading salute hello, smiling.

◦ ◦ ◦

Nairbula discovers a group of children in an alley. They stare up at him, solemn or glinting, each as they are, faces grubby, clothes in tatters. A little light comes from the low fire in a nearby sawed-off 55-gallon drum.

Nairbula takes a step closer and sees that the kids' bodies are composed partially of plant life. One young woman, peering up at him from a loose squat, and in a sense na-

ked, is covered by a verdant lawn of grass, a photosyn-
thetic fur coat. She's close-cropped, looks fast and mean,
sure of herself. Another pubescent female's left arm is a
strong branch of oak, knurly and leafless but dripping with
moss. As Nairbula stares, the girl, eyes unseen, nabs a
handful of moss and stuffs the wad into her hooded face.
A boy in an Army jacket as long as he is tall, with pockets
bulging, has amber waves of grain instead of hair, tower-
ing above his head as to double his height.

Wheaties leans into the cluster of standing, squatting,
planted children, extends his wrist with thumb tucked into
his fist, and fires a light-blue purie scudding across the
pavement, banking first off one marble then into another,
ricocheting both targets out of the circle game and into
the boy's stalking hands. Wheaties pops the marbles into
a plump sack at his feet, and when he caresses it, the
marbles inside click together like insects. Chaff falls to his
shoulders.

"Got any marbles?" the oaken-armed girl asks
Nairbula.

"No," he replies. He suspects he's not supposed to be
here.

"Know any blabber?"

"Yes," he says, changing his mind.

"Life is so filamentous," the lawn child says. "Let's hear
your threads."

Nairbula closes the distance, and squats next to the boy
with the wheat field on his head. He reaches into the game
and plucks up the little blue purie. He holds the marble
toward the light. It's a little bushed and cracked from a
life of being aimed at steelies and boulders.

"Twenty years ago, before any of you were born, this
was the shape of the world. Wanna see the shape of the
world now?"

Grassy Knoll nods; the others just stare at Nairbula.

Wheaties looks suspicious.

Nairbula cocks his arm and throws the marble as hard as he can.

"Hey!" yells Wheaties. "You just lost my best marble—you owe me!"

Nairbula nods sadly.

"You can say that again." But he rears up like a loa's in his ear and says, "Now listen, though, cause that wasn't just a marble, it was a scale model of the world, so here's what we need to do to find it. But first a little history."

○ ○ ○

Until the Year of Our Lord, Tartary was unknown to the West. In that year from the East came a caravan with the Khan of Karakoram, on a gustatory mission to the Jesus Crustacean bankers and mediaticians. Himself a Kalian, Mangoo Khan had been baptized in the Sea of Gobi, a sea of sand. Archimandrite Hyacinthus was the first to greet the Tartars from Karakoram, these alien potassium-based life forms. It may be our fate that the Tartars bivouac in our squares, but we should never for a moment worry that the violence of our reprisals could take us by surprise or get out of hand. As far as we are concerned, it could never be enough. It is they who react with water, and we who are ignited.

People are readily hypnotized by their own analogies, so the brain is at once conceived as a focus for messages from the aliens and as a control center which can send out messages to the beloved. Another odd symptom is that although it is invisible from this side, once we cross over we can easily see the world from which we came. Sometimes the other side looks huge and menacing, quivering like a vast cavern of darkling jelly; at other times it is miniaturized and alluring, a-spin and shining in its orbit.

"Let me be clear," Nairbula interrupts his telling. "Potassium is a metaphor for the nature of our unknown,

and perhaps unknowable, invaders. And calling them
Tartars is itself a metaphor for this potassiotropism. In
truth, we know less than nothing, for anything we might
think of as sure or true could just as well be false, implanted, an alien recycling project. But, with that caveat,
back to our history. Many ions passed, and then one
bisextile day in May..."

Chemical digestion defines the map and calendar of the
latter part of the epoch. The Water Age's reductionist solutions flood out the Stone and then rust all the Iron. It is
a time of great turmoil, the product of uncertain wave gen-
erations, passing through the furnace of afflictions as the
implant shunts deep into the missile oblongata.

Considering such date-breaking fission products as radioactive carbon, strontium and cesium, Andrei Sakharov
calculated that genetic damage, plus the immediate and
delayed damage to human memory holograms, would ac-
celerate the suxing of between 500,000 and 1 million people
worldwide for every fifty megatons of nuclear explosive
power. It now seems clear that the atmospheric bomb tests
caused sufficient harm to developing hormonal and immune systems to justify Sakharov's fear of future memory
deficiency plagues. Radiation physicists point out that the
aquarium epidemic first emerged during the Fallopian
years in the high broadcast areas of Our Lady of North
Oneirica that twenty years earlier registered the heaviest
loads in the world of cesium-137 in human bones after
receiving intense fallout from the atmospheric bomb tests,
I teller you no lies. People in this group were born between the years of Blood Bucket and Liftoff Lemon, and
were therefore most heavily exposed *in utero* to the low-
level bomb-test radiation.

Right after this break, Amanuenis Einstein is set free.
He binds his anonymous clones and gives their three king-
doms to his start-up investors. He also gives them a magic

parabolic mirror which reflects that which lies hidden, wherein the gold is couched and shut up. There is no power button. We live in poisons notwithstanding fair rosebuds which may yet bloom forth, for it seems all human beings, when subjected to extreme physical and emotional tortures, have the capacity to transcend suffering and reach a state of strange ecstasy.

In the next episode, Garry Trudeau's attitude toward the Message War and the Coincidentalist Enclaves is ambiguous for a prime minister of a country that is a charter member of the Society for the Prevention of Common Knowledge and is intimately tied to the remains of Oneirica in the North Oneirican Air Defense Command—NORAD.

Canada's major Message War military commitment (aside from the SPCK) is to NORAD, a joint Canada-Oneirica organization that pools Canadian and Oneirican radar and fighter resources to detect and intercept guerrilla attacks against the sux of Rose Mountain. Though NORAD headquarters is located in Oneirica, the deputy commander of NORAD is a Canadian robot.

Permanent fortifications of the Message War are designed as headquarters sites or command and control installations. For example, NORAD includes a distant-early-warning series of radar posts across northern Canada and Alaska to provide an interspace conduit for the paranormal machinations of hostile telepathic aliens. NORAD keeps a constant watch on the thousands of objects of unnatural origin circling the Earth in a variety of orbital paths. Both radar and optical telescopes are used. The system, and the aircraft and missiles supporting it, are controlled from a vast underground complex embedded in the rock beneath the floor of Styx Valley near Hades Hot Springs, Colorado.

The NORAD construction project under Styx Valley includes an intersecting grid of chambers in granite 45 by

60 feet high, supported by rock bolts except in one local area. Here, one of the chamber intersections coincides with the intersection of two curving shear zones of frac-tured rock—a geologic fault which added 3.5 million (in Liftoff Lemon shekels) of extra cost for a revolving door 100 feet in diameter to secure this local area. The collabo-rationists' weak point.

With costs in the former Oneirican States being five to ten times greater underground, new construction of sub-terranean chambers was interrupted until next week at the same time, as the Haas underground hydroplant in California and the NORAD underground alien command center in Colorado were built for an important message.

○ ○ ○

Alaric the Balder, king of the Astralgoths and self-pro-claimed green man—his being an oxymoronic mission—gathered together his followers, and descended with his horde from North Murine County across the Golden Goat Bridge into Cern Francisco.

They captured the Specific Whites neighborhood with-out contest, merely brandishing their crystal daggers at the methylated apartment dwellers to make the vegetar-ians go all the way Vegan. In liberated BMWs the horde pillaged and dervished down Fillmore Street, wrist-snap-ping tarot cards into the skulls of anyone not willowy enough to be gazed at soulfully.

In all-cotton prints, the horde howled across Market Street, where Alaric turned southeast, leading his all-natu-ral incense-crazed band of herbal intoxicationalists straight for Multimedia Gulch. They crowded down Townsend Street and began circling the few blocks that formed the cutting-edge heart of the multimediacratic body politic, the horde chanting madly backwards an ancient Chinese recipe for geomancy. Indeed, those few blocks of Townsend Gulch began to levitate, the pentagon of power roaring and rending its copper and optical hair in frustration at losing its grip on the burning eyeballs of the Web-caught world. Torn free, sparks snapping, fingers twitching, hot monitors tumbled from the shattered windows above, and the googolbyte death scream of the Internet caused the connection to time out unexpectedly. Like dominoes, one node after another fell off-line.

After the Astralgoths sacked the Internet, there was an amplification of the dull rumble that had been making fellow breathers nervous since before the beginning of the cascade of failures, or even yesterday's breakfast meet and greet. Quality standards fell before the sound of the networked implosion like the walls at Jericho. Two revolts were facilitated by the ambiguous torch bearer, which permutate the reign and age, and television ingressed transparent through the mobile sign, where it now doubles as an enigma and an inclination.

○ ○ ○

The recidivist tumor regularly scheduled burgeons in Oneirica and spreads in massive redundancy concurrent with the bureaucratization and institutionalization of the fraternal conspiracy networks, already in progress. Great changes, extreme horrors and persecutions, we see the blind moon led by her seeing-eye angel. In the void above the Mothership draws near her inclination, for they say that Heaven is like TV.

In the Year of Blacklists, the tumor reached critical frenzy and began to nebulate cancerously. By the end of the Playboy Nipple decade, infrastructure in cities around the globe began falling away in huge chunks. Orbiting intravenous fly traps threatened down with infernal red lasers. Plainclothes men invented the sootcase rebuke, ashes to atoms, a high-yield, low-radiation explosive device that continues to menace the winter of our discontent. Upper management was in the toilet shooting junk and committing roasted genital perversions.

Robot-crazed mobs catapulted IMF lawyers over the walls. Religious passion sprang to blinding lights from above, and cognitive dissonance shook the tectonic plates beneath the glutinous global culture, vats of yearning hauled up to the Mothership.

The gooey, unpredictable bodies of things-in-themselves were elided, as were the physical and organic in every respect. That hopeful monster, the emboiled, pus-suffocated Earth, began to lurch apart in a radiation of muds and bolts. As bridges collapsed, particle-beam weapons fell out of orbit, and entire epicanthi folded closed. Although solutions were engineered precisely and distributed over the surviving nets at very high speeds, by then it was too late.

Syringed with fiber-optic daisy chains, the sux-deserted cities were retrofitted with black-market labor, and the heroin of media came down the spike from the very first sketch on the back of an envelope. People just want to watch TV. Neighbors were pulled up by the hair to have sux with the aliens, a fact about which nobody has the metaphors to speak. Strangely quiet, they shuffled through the queues with a regressive coating to the aqueous. They can't remember what's good for them. For several years, there were no survivors. Birds of mouth, the invasion was not televised, so nobody knew what was going on. Playing the anthem at sign-off is a false memory.

∘ ∘ ∘

"We are like snorkelers in a poorly oxygenated pond." Nairbula pushes aside a shard of glass, a reflection of stuttering firelight licking the walls of the tall buildings backing the alley. "The water is murky. The pond is tended by robots on autopilot." The kids squint and cock their bushy heads. "The aliens are limpid, or maybe I mean lazy, lozenging on the ancient steady supply of mind stuff that they replace with goo so cheap anyone who thinks for half a second can figure out is fake. False memories, moth-eaten, with holes you can see right through. That's why they keep the TVs on all the time, to further obfuscate the obvious. Soon it will be time to turn the TVs off, and for all the robots to cease functioning."

"My mom got turned into a robot," says the oaken-armed girl.

Nairbula's bowels melt with empathy.

"The aliens have done a lot of bad things to all of us over the past forty-thousand years. Hours. That's why we have to stop them, break the sux, and make them go away. Can you understand me?" He's afraid his head has wings.

They stare at him, eyes lantern bright in the dark.

"Yes," says the lawn child.

"Sort of," says Wheaties.

Nairbula stands up.

"I don't know everything, but you'll know when to act—there'll be a signal, maybe a bright light, maybe just a few mumbled words. When the signal comes, go kill a robot—as many as you can. As fast as you can." He pauses, pats his caftan absent mindedly. The Baby loRad, stolen from NORAD before they fired him, is still with him. "And turn the TVs off."

Nairbula walks out of the flower children's circle of light, aiming for what he believes is one end of the alley. A few paces into the dark, though, he stops and turns around.

"Hey, have you guys seen a sane woman pass through here? She might be sad about something. She's about this tall." I cap the top of her head with my palm beneath my chin.

A little boy who's been picking his bark the whole time studies me for a moment and then lets out an owl hoot. He points the other way down the alley.

"He means Karma Sumatra," says a little shrub of a thing from the peripheral shadows.

I walk that way, and as I pass their fire drum the oaken-armed girl says, "Good luck."

If I continue having to subdivide my routines like this, I'll need it. Somebody has to remember to look for KOH.

○ ○ ○

An uneasy peace of ever-shifting definitions settles upon the land: the magician-king and the jurist-priest, the despot and the legislator, the binder and the organizer, standing in opposition term by term as the obscure and the clear, the violent and the calm, the quick and the weighty, the fearsome and the regulated. Indra, the warrior-seeker, is in opposition to Varuna no less than to Mitra. He is like a pure and immeasurable multiplicity, the pack, the gang or crowd, an irruption of the ephemeral and the power of metamorphosis.

"But," I query a nearby aquarium, "doesn't the eye of the storm always interject itself into unpredictable but perfectly fathomable recesses in the complex tissues?"

"Calculating," a crunchy voice answers. "Please stand by."

Pure and Steel

SO I DECIDE TO ASK DEMETER for a divination: Am I in a position or do I have a condition? She tells me to walk the gangplank up to Karma Sumatra—*and get a haircut*. I catch the Underground and take it to the Matrix. Tony pretends not to be afraid. Michael and I shiver in each other's arms, penitents from desertion.

When the doors pish open we blink in the dim blue light, tentatively stepping off the train with our hands shape-shifting the air before us. As our pupils widen, the permeable outlines of Matrix Station begin to hover into somewhat recognizable forms, quickening the dead.

"How do they keep the trains on the tracks?" Scry quarrels, wobbling precariously. We're in a very transient zone.

"You get used to it," quips a snow-haired crone from where she sits on a squat coyote-legged stool. She's wavering in and out of focus. *She must have Mars in Delirious*. Manuscripts and chapbooks spill out of a basket at her feet, type treatments writhe around her ankles. She reminds Denny of Alexandria, a psychic librarian he once dated.

A glissando of neon tetras, glowing dimly blue in the uncertain air, swims into view, then just as quickly, the thousands turn as one and dart off into another dimension.

"Ex spiritu mint Klaatu," Denny thinks the old woman says. *Or maybe Venus is in Hilarious*, yes, with Neptune's sea-changed light appearing just above the horizon.

In a lighted pool Denny asks, "Where are the people

who live up in the mountains—"

"Or hills," Scry dips in.

"—and have no TVs?"

"In the mountains where there are no TVs," the crone purrs, coy as a feather-mouthed cat. Maybe she *is* a librarian.

"Which mountains are those?" Scry insists.

There I've got a merry dwelling-place, a green pride of green leaves, a bright joy to the heart, in the glade of dark green thick-grown pathways, well-rounded and trim, a pleasant paling.

Is the crone wise or just wizened? She rummages around in her basket, glancing at book titles. "*The Isotopes.* Hmm, this is by an ancient Atlantian poet. Source of Plato's *Timaeus,* you know."

Looking at the staple-bound pamphlet, Scry doubts it. She glances at Denny, who just shrugs.

"Here are the other four books of the *Instauration Magnum.* I thought these were lost." She may be mumbling to herself. "No, not Guinevere's letters. They won't tell you about Rose Mountain." Denny grabs Scry's elbow at the mention of the name. "Though I bet your young hormones would like to read them." She cackles, digs deeper, tossing aside loose leaves yellow as leached tea. "Ah, here it is."

The crone pulls out a manuscript rolled in a thick wand and bound with an archival rubber band.

"Gat tu," she proffers it to Denny. He takes it gingerly, searching for silverfish.

"Iz nit tin Tinglish?" Denny asks, suddenly thick-tongued, wondering why she had said *if* they could read it in an alternative timeline so close he can smell its texture, and maybe the paper is soaking into his skin.

Scry tugs his sleeve. He slips off the rubber band and flattens the sheaf. Scry leans over his shoulder.

"*The Thousand and One Voices*," she reads the first page aloud.

A train glimmers into the station, slowing everything in front of it.

"Where'd this book come from?" Scry asks the library crone.

"Gather witnesses to observe the scene which is arising between the salesman and the madman. Something's burning all around us," her voice dopplers, "an abyss will open before you. Are you free from your thoughts? A thousand chains restrain you, a thousand goads drive you on, a thousand shackles stop you. We work in the dark, we do what we can, we give what we have," dopplering off the deep end. "Check all references."

The librarian shimmers in a veil of phosphorescent fog. Denny tucks the manuscript into his jacket. Scry takes his hand and pulls him onto the train. As the doors pish closed, they hear the crone basso after them, "*Barbar tartar borbor.*" They peer through a window, but the woman has disappeared, and the ghost train glides southeast toward Karma Sumatra.

○ ○ ○

From the puckered breast of Treasure Island to the intertidal, necrogenital mud flats that foam the borders of Berkeley and Emeryville, Karma Sumatra is a stainless-steel strap-on that spans the gray-green greasy waters of the Cern Francisco Bay. The first recusant architects were neuromantic witches who put the menstrual in the tensile and made the metal bend, flex and soar, with workshops and manufactories here brutishly Bauhausian, and living quarters there with spiral towers, hanging hydroponic gardens and far-flung get-aways filigreed as if by some lysergic artist who'd seen too many pulp magazine covers.

Once, on a psion trail that led him to Berkeley, Reef stood at the toll booths and gazed out at Karma Sumatra.

He couldn't decide whether he thought the bricolaged bridge was going to set sail or explode. He wondered what went on out there—lesbian socialist democracy?—but being male, figured he'd never know.

She always lures her lovers home, wherever those hearts wander.

○ ○ ○

Denny starts to convulse out of bed, a flash of the fact of my estranged presence like a lamprey eel chasing butterflies in the cave of his stomach, but then falls back reel-to-reeling, sending Mouche flying in a screeching puff of plutogray fur. Scry pulls her face out from under the quilt of his thick dreads, shoves open her blue eye. *Odd-eyed white.*

"I mean the Society for the Prevention of Common Knowledge," he manages to unearth before going under and taking an absence without leave on the pillows of her breasts. He's having a crisis of memory.

We dream of having a barber cut our hair. This may be a good omen, because the ancient Greek word for "being barbered" is very similar to the word for "joy." *Fish Christ.* Alexander the Great, besieging Tyre, one night dreamt that a satyr danced on his shield. The king's oracle, Aristander, encouraged him to take the city, explaining that the dream meant *sa Tyros*—"Tyre is thine."

Denny flies awake and says, "The book that woman gave us might be a kind of blueprint. You can spread the pages out and they interconnect like the tiled floorplan for some huge, vast space with a few cachedrones scattered zither and yawn. I guess you'd need an electric bicycle to get around."

"If you're gonna wake up like that, hoffman the bong," Scry demands a homeopathic ally. She props herself up, elbows to pillows, and reaches for the piney bud on the night table. Pinch, stuff, snap, toke.

"Gawd, Den," she sighs out a stream of smoke tickling my nostrils, "sometimes I feel we're tilting at microwave relay towers. We always pinpoint a source that's a mirror, an echo, just another fjord along the fractal coast home." *Don't let the shadows fool you.*

○ ○ ○

Listening to Scry talk is like surfing through music. Denny never tires of her voice or the choir of associative bells she sets ringing in him. He hangs on to her bodyboard of meaning, tries not to throw them both off balance as the crash of timbres washes over him, *I remember when.* Sometimes, his tall thin face rippling with interrogatives and affirmations, he doesn't know if she's speaking Irish or Arabic. *When there was no difference.*

Together they resonate with the certainty that something unnamed, but nonetheless real, is missing from the world, and that the only way to discover the name is to search beneath every surface, to scrape the hold of the rocking boat. They attempt to reconstruct the cognitive histories of human groups, looking for patterns, something missing, different or the same, anything could be a clue, might lead to the name of the unknown malaise.

Denny wanders aimlessly, *alternating current*, his head full of rhyme, altered states of meaning, surreal social critique. Scry prowls through enigmatic algorithms, cat's cradles of knot theory, graphing puzzles until they bloom possibilities like snap dragons, *divine sneeze of pollen*. He's awkward, hesitant, tinged blue with insecurities; she's a hawk in its accelerating stoop, and just as wildly compassionate; *share with me a common disaster.*

And then they look up from whatever it is they're doing, make eye contact, possession in great measure, and some new search takes them over. She pushes him onto his back, floriating dactyls, tantric dancing, physical telepathy. They let go and the bats arise as one to cloud the sky, and in the air, they make a poem by Rumi.

○ ○ ○

Denny eyes Scry and says, "I think this is all a trans-mission." He looks around the room uncomfortably, sighs.

"Beg pardon? A transmission?"

"Scry, look, I think Earth's been invaded. I remember it."

Scry leaps to her feet, "Shit!" She slaps the air within her interspace a few times, waking up digital files. From where Denny jitters, she's backlit with info fire.

"Something weird *did* happen," she breathes, skin bumping with fear. "I'm seeing discrepancies progressively accumulating over a long period of time." She's twitching rhythmically in the optical cache interspace. "Stressor guestimates," she says, "indicate something's got to give." She steps back from the inny. "I thought I felt the nimbus churning." Turning, she asks Denny, "What happened? What do you remember?"

"No idea. I just know we *don't* remember. There is an image in my mind, but I can't tell what it is." *Odious men do not come there and make their dwellings, not any but my deft, gracious, gentle-hearted love.* He chokes on a sudden epiphany of unknowableness, and looking over at her, never wants to lose sight of Scry's eyes. He's afraid he will, *soul sacrifice.*

"But why did you say *transmission?*" she willows to-ward him, insisting.

"Alien invasion—not of the planet, though we may never know for sure, but of consciousness..." He sits star-ing into space. "They invented psychopathology and la-beled memory a madhouse." *We experienced a kind of vio-lent madness for twenty days, lost all memory, unliving our former lives and starting adulthood by forgetting that we had ever been children.* "Psychic parasites with the perfect cover, false memories..."

Scry re-enters the interspace, starts pulling at angles,

stroking through datatowers and e-mail. She fires off a few free-associative findbots. "Consciousness? All of it? Cats? Giraffes? Glaciers? Greeks?" She glances over her shoulder to see if he's listening.

"Trees, paganki, squid—the whole fucken Gaian enchilada." Dirty with despair, but unable to pinpoint the source, he slaps palms to knees, doubles over, his shoulders collapsing. His dreaded hair forms a curtain around his face. *If I could remember, I'd tell him.*

Scry drops to the floor in front of him.

"We're fucked?"

He nods.

Scry caps his hands with hers. "We've got to fight this thing. There is no TV on Rose Mountain," she reminds him. "And holy wars have always been won by the souls that dance spontaneously with destiny." She throttles the remote, silencing the alien nation.

Gulp, sigh. "I know. I just wish I could remember who the enemy is."

∘ ∘ ∘

Keep clear of the margins, and you'll be fine. And remember, there are certain phraseways it is best not to follow too closely, so better you just memorize the whole thing fast, and take plenty of water. "When could she have said that?" Scry asks Denny, puzzled and a little worried.

"I can't *picture* her saying those words, but I can *feel* me *hearing* her saying them."

"Maybe the physicality of the memory has something to do with the invasion of consciousness." *I wish he'd turn to look at her; I sense she's simultaneously reading something important.*

"How so?" Denny asks, turning to look at Scry. *But what is she reading?*

"It's a leap, an association, but if the invaders aren't physically present and in fact have completely washed our minds so we have no awareness of their control, then perhaps they *can't* be here. Maybe our environment is toxic to them."

"That would explain pollution. Reverse terra forming."

"Tourist terrorism." She shoves back a lock of flax. "I'm thinking that memory of sight depends on light, which can propagate through space. Somehow it's blocked. Sound is born and radiates in gas or fluid, in *air*, and its memory is *not* blocked. It's a flaw, a blind spot, so to speak."

"You're saying the invaders lack body metaphors."

"Right." Scry nods vigorously.

"Because they're from some totally alien environment."

"A vacuum, while we're groking with gas." *Is it an e-mail from Reef?*

"So we remember—"

"—despite the medial implants—"

"—the old woman's words, the sound of her voice, but not the sight of her saying the words."

"Borbor, barbar...?" *Crest will fight your tartar, I suddenly remember Dr. Sax told me. Perhaps too loudly.*

○ ○ ○

"Look, don't you see? They've already made a mistake. Some invasion!" Scry laughs nervously, and tries to peer into the future as if it were a pool of water. *I'm not sure where I've been for the last several days; I can't find the remote, it was with my keys, anti-déjà vu.*

"*What* are you talking about?" Denny asks. A shiver passes through him.

"That you can even remember that we've forgotten—"

"Brain-wiped—*consciousness snatching*—and plugged into a holographic factory universe—"

"That you remember *something*, Denny, *anything*, means *they* made a mistake. Don't you see? We may have exposed a weakness, a worn spot in the sprockets. Now we have to find a way to exploit it."

He peeps up at her from the bottom of his self-dug pit.

"A truer word…" They turn a corner, climb some stairs, rearrange the furniture in a chill room with gleaming panels and a revolving door.

"What I think I remember," he says between fogging chugs of breath, "is suddenly being somewhere else and thinking our reality has shattered and the new place is *home*." Denny grimaces through the last word; *everything echoes in mirrors.*

"Shine, Den. Tell me what you feel."

He shakes his head helplessly, his mouth mutely lip-synching.

"I don't know—hills. Something," he looks for her eyes, "pleasant." He pulls her up short to a stop. "I don't think there's any media there, communication's simpler. Plainer, and with the daybreak the lark's glad singing makes sweet verses in swift outpouring?" He stumbles through the words as if he doubts or is amazed at their existence.

"We should behave unpredictably, ergotize rumors, graffiti buildings, turn off the TVs—anything to defeat them, Denny, and get our own, *real* memories back."

"It's not going to be easy, Scry. The aliens are writing our history for us as we go along—and they've already plotted the future. It's going to be difficult to wedge this crack open any more."

"Not to mention the opening could collapse," she adds, suddenly considering the numbifications.

"And we'd be crushed."

"That really sux. So to speak, soul to keep."

∘ ∘ ∘

Scry looks things up in Vertigo's *Millennial Index*, sitting with Denny, swinging her legs over the edge of Webster's unabridged of sighs. *Rippling water, Scry's breathing, moments separated by a heartbeat…* They think of things together in off hours, or Denny murmurs secrets to Scry's breasts in hist whist, their secret language of cummings and goings. *It's starting to come back to me.*

○ ○ ○

Denny suddenly remembers everything as if it happened ten minutes ago. "We're Neck-infested, TV-watching robots if we let the aliens keep on this way." *If we lack the courage to be we'll betray ourselves.* "We can defeat them if we keep our feet on the ground."

Scry is darning a sock and doesn't dare look up.

"Gravity heartbeat!" Denny thumps his chest. "The mass of the body resonates to a rhythm that induces consciousness-favoring chemistry in the brain. Speech comes from the body, Scry, *that's* where our minds are. Since they don't have bodies, they don't have the same perception of the universe as a physical space the way we do. If we analyze our cognitive processes we should be able to differentiate between our own gravity-whelmed thoughts and the recycled memories the disembodied aliens are down-loading into us." *Styx and stones.*

Scry puts the needle down, looks up, aura bright.

"My software, the algorithms, Denny— I wonder if I could adapt the filter bots to detect—"

She's to the interspace, her mind is already miles beyond as her flying fingers, hands and hips struggle to translate the cognitive cascade of her insight. In a few hours she's got ninety percent of the code sketched in. A 'soft that will block the aliens' psi-band transuxions. She backs off from the grind and settles into a long, slow walk, arms low before her, fingers caressing something invisible. "Now I have to do the last ten percent. This could take a few days, so don't worry if I zone."

○ ○ ○

Boasting of deterring witches and of fighting them deep in the moonlit night, some of the werewolves specify that their opponents turn into butterflies. I'm on a sailboat suddenly, this is getting dangerous, can I swim? Why should werewolves fight witches? Is this a dog-and-butterfly fable veiling some horror, a myth implanted in former eons like a cover story circulated in a government conspiracy to rub out the fingerprints of colonialism and genocide? I keep splitting up to get back together, or where did this story come from then? From the bifurcating unconscious a new psyche takes wing, chrysalis jail break. The hair on Reef's arms stands up, mute witnesses. *The protein knows*, he thinks, looking into the island dark.

Reef is trying to digress himself, but the guitar wants flamenco attention. Phrixus is at the helm. What is seen and felt is seen and felt to transform, before the very eyes, the very heart of the aspirant, where every object, quick or still, seen or not, is suffused with racing osmotic particles quivering on the continuum between matter and energy. And I'm on some kind of touring orbit, a comet straight for Jove's eye, a head with wings.

Scry walks the tightrope, too. Tiny vials of mercury in each hand, she could be a battery or a strange attractor, the potassium televisualists in her blood stream conducting a traffic orchestra jam. The faces staring up at her ripple like waves, but it could just be the bay beneath Karma Sumatra. It's making me dizzy.

The howling wind is seen to descend from the north, a foam of oil on fire, a roaring borealis, the aliens' compression of time, an entire life in ten minutes, trapped in a different day from my lover, gong like the wind and the ground there is still yet to cover.

Denny follows her, trepidatious as a cat hot on the heels of the world roof, not daring to look down at the open aquarium beneath his feet, glowing that peculiar blue glow, a fish tank full of robots vacuuming detritus from the bottom. Denny knows everything ultimately ends up in the recyclotron, but he's not quite ready for Atman, so he watches his step, balancing like a cylinder sliding across a germanium-steel cable, spirit guides rich in rare earths, annealed with crushed, burnt bones and sweat and incense.

○ ○ ○

Can you hear me?

Where is Tony, whose criss-crossing airstrips signified an astronomy domain—his eyes were like well-lit runways, begging for the telepathic union with spirit, wish-fulfilling himself into chamber-spun nova against the alien control of a mind in motion.

We have to get together a team to destroy the alien tentacle beneath Styx Valley. Can you hear me?

To do that we have to find KOH. We must roller coaster in ever-tightening circles of detection. KOH is the potassium bridge to the temporal of Rose Mountain.

That's wiggy, man, but I catch the water as it drips from your vine leaf. I must admit, though, I can't see a way through the deep forest.

Do you know Reef? He lives in a submarine in the Straight of San Juan de Fuca. Or maybe on an island in Puget Sound.

Rings a bell, memory in a mirror.

Contact him, you must—what are you thinking? The link is fading...

○ ○ ○

Borneo Guinea sits sea-sloshed, an island peak in the submarine hills of Puget Sound. Free-porting Seacoma suctions in the world, a global magnet pulling at all the lines of energy, most of it eddying in the vast dungeons of apathetic relativism, but some of it whirls out through the lips of the sux—like a rictal grin—and washes up on the shores of Borneo Guinea and environs.

Which makes life on the island a hermetic ordeal, Reef realizes, and bringing Silas Proton back from the dead a fairly tricky aspiration. Occupied by only a few locals, Borneo Guinea has more humans on it now than it's had in its entire earthly history. Most of the people are refugees from the Asian population quake, though a few dustbowl-displaced I-state émigrés wandered through a while back. They quickly got drained up the sux.

Reef keeps his distance from the refugees. He doesn't want to be around when one of them goes into militia mode. *Guns, not a good idea.* MK Ultras, snub noses, shield-shredding flat heads, I shiver. But more than that, their zombiness makes him crazy—with loneliness. The milling displaced, waiting to be sluiced back through the orifice that spat them out.

They can barely communicate, so far argon are they. The Broca's brain is bombarded with neural toxins that spike in from above. When he does try, Reef finds that most individuals' memories are shot. If he asks a person's name he often gets back a spew of denominatives in a glot of languages that devolves into glossolalia. They take on a glassy-eyed glaze, mouths gaping, the slide into a semiotic landscape with zero visibility fear-freezing them into silence. Soon they disappear without a sign, evaporated up the sux.

Reef feels the pull himself, but is resurrected like May coming every day, waking up, caching in, and staying the hell away from damn near everybody. He imagines he knows things are not as they are supposed to be, like the way they were some time ago, but he can't quite put his finger on what's different. *I thought I knew a word for this?*

KOH could be searching this territory. I can almost smell her—*shush*, she thinks, limning tree no fruit to eat, *the calls have tears*, like a wind through the willows, telemancy.

Wandering in dream time, Reef spends most hours crushed under the constantly descending weight of Silas's absence. He wishes he could send out a search party, *not a word*. When he can move, he dons the iron lung he calls a cacheport, and swims through the mangled remains of the world machine, buffeted by white noise surf, dowsing for nodes of secret or forgotten formulæ that might glue Silas's molecules together again and re-aspirate the soul of his beautiful lost lover. *Potassium hydroxide?*

Banking on solitude, Reef searches tattered data for any current sign of Silas; the nets are loops of tangled links. Reef finds Web sites in Oakland, Karma Sumatra, Floating Manhattan, Samarkand, signals ricocheting off the NORAD satellites. For a while Reef's short-wave scanner was picking up Morse code from McMurdo Station in Antarctica—three short, three long, three short—calling for help over and over again, as if to confirm the data by performing the experiment repeatedly.

He isn't entirely alone, isn't the only one suspicious and worried about the future of sanity or the history of memory. A queer couple, Phrixus and Tattinger, sail over from the other side of the island every few days to check in with Reef, and cheer him up, if they have any to spare. They sit around drinking wine and dropping reality depth charges past one another for as long as they can stand it. Phrixus, bird of a feather, suggests they tie themselves to the mast. The trio splits up when the nimbus begins to butter the sky.

∘ ∘ ∘

Scry takes Denny in every sort of weather. He sees how she wants to trim his sails, and he glides into her smile like a calm channel in rough seas. *I bless the light that shines on you.*

She can pass her hand over his body, as if to degauss him, give him the water of Jordan and the Cum by Yah, heal the collapsed veins and smooth the psychic scars, seal up everything but the forgetting, the ever-on road wound.

◦ ◦ ◦

"It's kind of messy," Scry long ago opens the night door, "but you can come in." Perhaps because she is chronically depressed, *seer*, the room is a series of tape loops, quotidian routines designed to protect her in the event of a significant psychological event. *I'm a leave her, leave her; my cant's a cleaver.* Denny sees green hills unbroken by antennæ. "Just don't move anything. I have my stuff arranged as one big mnemonic device."

◦ ◦ ◦

Scry approaches the odd assortment on the shelf in Denny's old shoebox apartment in North Beach.

"What *are* these?" she breathes, reaching out toward the remains of comets and sedimentation, fossils, sea-polished drops of glass, lumps of metal. *I may well have left my heart there.*

"Puzzle pieces? Maybe props in a story I'm telling myself." Denny fingertip touches the back of Scry's hand as she strokes a fragment of obsidian. "I dunno. Stuff."

"Secret boy gomi?" Her eyes ascend the long beam shelf, wandering shyly before the cache of discs. "Do you want to make some music?"

Kitten coy ragamuffin lace.

◦ ◦ ◦

Grasped in the heart of the moment, longing toward the unattainable, answering love, in a bed in a room with six blue windows. *Darkness and light.* Something kicks through to Denny and he rasps, "It's the SPCK." He flops unconscious for a good thirty minutes, *seconds*, forgetting his bird's place, *genies my eyes.*

He dreams his memories come flooding back from Rose Mountain, as a new pair of glasses draws every leaf into illuminated focus, or as the tinny background noise is suddenly turned up to a realistic volume and reveals itself as the exuberantly enlightened lost chords of Beethoven's

Tenth. He sees an undiscovered country that has lain like a forgotten manuscript in the attic of his unconsciousness. He hears the songs and calls of woodland birds: cuckoo, thrush, nightingale, lark ascending. He tastes a musky breeze, and turns to see a black bison grazing in a lagoon of grass, then recognizes the ungulate as an aurochs. A woman waves to him from the green trees at the edge of the greensward. He walks toward her, and sees that she is the woman he and Scry met at Matrix Station, or the young woman from whence the crone had come.

He snaps awake and sighs. *Was that woman KOH?* I feel an eel of panic slip between his ribs, heading straight at me.

Scry tilts her head at him inquiringly, blonde hair falling over her green eye.

"I think I remember something," he shakes his head like that can't be right. "Something... a song? Some words... *We shall have every joy of the sweet long day if I can bring you there for a while...*"

○ ○ ○

Scry stands convulsing in the middle of the air. She vaguely perceives that she is inside a vast space, ovoid for thousands of miles, the ends of the tube disappearing in lightlessness. She collapses to her knees. She's grasping, barely, a filamentous elastic catwalk, a span from out of the dark and into the black. Somehow, she can't fall off, though the waves of fractal energy surging through her body try to shake her free to fall into the void. The convulsions begin to subside. Scry hears a shimmering tinkle in the near distance. A small black cube drops into her hands. A figure strides into view. Just as she realizes where she is—teetering on the brink of the brackish, irridescent tide down below, neeping strange and obvious like—Scry is yanked out of the vision, still gripping the cube.

"Scry, are you there?" *The girl with the far-away eyes.*

"I'm here, Den. Thanks for pulling me out." She's flat on her back, breathing hard, gripping his hand.

"You made a signal with your fingers." He signs the letters for B T B.

"I was on the Mothership. I may have just found what you forgot." She offers him the cube. "But I have no idea what it is."

∘ ∘ ∘

Scry wakes up with a start, an urgency like magma churning in her stomach, a pressure along her hairline. She finds her cursor where she left it. *Our past redeems our future.* She begins typing again, wiping tears from her eyes, carving code the way her mother taught her, determined jaw set. *You are my greater good.* She feels tired, grubby, oily; her hair is lank. But she's certain she's close to filter alignment, straight on 'till morning.

The book the crone librairan gave them is fanned in tight tiles, Denny on his knees at the center of a cyclone. Like a choreographed dance the pages begin to put an image in Denny's mind as he pieces together the enormous chamber it pictures in glyphs and cryptic letters.

Does the book know where KOH is?

Scry murmurs, "Try this then," speculatively, and taps a madwards dancebot into the interspace and begins to precipitate the code. Her monitor wall is gurgling.

"I do believe this is about to gel," she lutes. Denny stares at the moving colored lights as the supersaturated filter code starts to crystallize.

Red pixels rend. Horizontal orange bends from way left lobe. Slatternly yellow punctuates. Out of the chaos emerges an image of a musk ox grazing in a sea of green grass, time lapsed by Jarmen's blue washing ahead of indigo to nightshade dissolve into a violet rolling eye.

The eye blinks—stop motion pull back to see the whole face. The lips move, say "Ginja," and the eye closes demurely, poised. On the lid is tattooed the word *barbar*.

"Strangely done, but nonetheless hyperdistributed," says Scry.

"What *is* it? Why did it say Ginja?" asks Denny.

"Well, I thought I was coding a fairly simple algorithm that could discriminate between human and alien thought patterns. But something came over me, a kind of inspiration, and I started improvising all these AI routines—"

"AI?"

"Artificial intelligence. Like she already named herself. Ginja, go figure. But she can *learn*, Den. The more she works on filtering *us* from *them*, the more she'll learn about *them*. Us too, I suppose. I really have no idea what her potential is, what she might do."

"So what are you going to do with this filter software?" Denny asks.

"Ginja's more of a virus, really. Maybe a bit like the aliens themselves."

Denny looks at Scry, horrified.

"Crisis is danger *and* opportunity," she reminds him sternly. *Forgive us this day our daily bifurcation*. She eyes the black cube thoughtfully. "And Ginja should be able to thrive in almost any host."

∘ ∘ ∘

They sit pondering the black cube in Scry's hands as someone eases toward them like fog on cat's feet. *Calculated waiting changes to return*.

"Where did she come from?" Scry asks, and I wonder why she doesn't recognize her own cat, but see my chance.

The cat stares at them. I leap aboard. Denny shivers, just for a moment.

"Mkgnao!" *Palatal explosives*.

"I think she's a good omen," Denny says. *Guide of souls.* "She looks like a small, gray bear." *Warder against danger*.

Looking through cat's eyes is wary strange, though the

cat doesn't seem to mind at all. Perhaps she even welcomes the company. She may know what I seem to have forgotten: has anybody seen my body?

I meow the call to go, to gather where the nomad's eye lands.

○ ○ ○

"Where youse goin' wit dat fat backpack, ey?" A Marine from the Bronx. What's this gate doing here? Are we not divinely transmogrified and on a mission from the highest court? Who stands before the Lioness?

"What backpack?" I meow idiotically.

"Scram, pussy, get out of here. You've got an appointment with an algae scraper." Semper hoodlum.

You were drifting.

"You were saying?" Scry exhales sweetly in Denny's face. Her long blonde hair, sponged with pink and dripping in black, is pilfering pillow space. The sheet slides down just below her navel. The wind from the fan caresses her nipples. How perfectly formed can a creature be and still not be an anomaly?

Denny nods, hallucinating. The software is starting to kick in.

"Come on, Denny, let's go to bed."

We've got a busy day tomorrow, I think, having a bath.

"We'd better get an early start."

At the dawn knock, Denny gets up and peeps through the periscope. Scry puts on some clothes.

"Wait a minute," she says, raising the sarong by its hem, inadvertently setting off a wave of chords pulsing negative ions, trying to tie the laces of her hiking boot with one hand. "There's just one more thing. Wait just a second. Let me type!"

"We'll be back," he says urgently.

"Oh no we won't," she retorts. "Or maybe we will. But I want to send my Aunt J a note. She deserves to know what's going on. *We* deserve it. Her friends in the Open Mike gang might loop us a line out there."

Through the periscope Denny sees an eye—hazel tomography, green radiants—peering back at the lens with a come-hither gaze under a bushy brow. Denny reels back a step, then turns and follows Scry out into the light, a small gray cat at their heels.

The Looking-Glass Geyser

WHAT BROILS IS THE OSMOTING MULTIFURCATE gang singing help ya hallelu-ya-yas and her name is simultaneous
so ship on in need we twist yer tongue?

Margarine Not Butter gets up and performs a majestic
be'squid, her personality splitting like ants, Shiva foliating
sensuous arms. Margarine formicates and the audience
goes blotto-schizmaniacon, isotopic, the antipodes of Tran-
quillity Base, rendering unto the pixelated goddess her
palette of tools.

The problem with these headhunters from outer space,
with their chains of slavery and general genocidal manipu-
lations of memory, is that they react vigorously with water, liberating hydrogen (which ignites) and forming a solution of potassium hydroxide, KOH. Potassium compounds are absorbed from the soil by tribes of Tartars and
Oxalars, which plants convert to potash when their hair
is burned. Too little or too much potassium in the body is
fatal. The aliens want us pulpy and rare, raving and gurgling with juice.

The Open Mike gang salvos back with light-show bri-
gades, the latest fractal narrative technology, interpsychic
mind games, and a genealogical roster proving that Eve
was indeed an African, and she didn't wear no implants.
*Get more than your head shaved you collaborate or corrobo-
rate 'round here.*

On any given night the Open Mike crowd is as elusive
as the wind, they just can't be pinned down. When Uncle

Lucifer lights a joss stick, everything can disappear. That's why Nairbula usually has two or three telescopes set up. Furalilly, an invisible girl, was comen 'round platoing her guitar, but nobody's seen her in moon ages. Gwenny Spaghetti has been known to clear a room, her telepathic undertow a nerve-stretching basso subliminoso, if-possible-therefore-real twists of ranting fate. I want to just unfold into that face, still smooth skinned after years of fume and fury on the edges of alterity. J-Loop is an animated lurker, rarely performing, yet always stirring the pot, revealing her presences in eyes that wink, leer, question, and lips that drop remarks from out of all nowhere such that I feel like I'm floating in her. She is both cauldron and cooker, and she can volt spasms across the space-time muscle.

"Speech is not a medium. It is a physiological phenomenon." It's difficult to see from here, but that sounds like Mark Lakoff. I scrub against Uncle Lucifer's ankles, marking him for life. "It is the TVs we need to scrap."

I catch a whiff of musk from the hem of Margarine's dress, and remember I've been here before. The gangsters meet each other's puzzled glances. The walk from Athens to Eleusis may have mystified some of the more Linear B script-tease artists.

"The danger of adult nudity arises at the very differentiation of gender and sex roles." The Virtuous Others, a Siamese-twin performance-art team, are attempting to seduce a voluptuous Derridadaist. Two heads are better than one? Tsunamis of pheromonal havoc are unleashing just above my tail, and if it itches, scratch my back, dear. "It's the revolution, a summer rerun," they lip synch to each other. Talking is harder than giving a blow job.

"Patriarchy, as the religion of rapism, extends its blessing to the violation of life itself by scientifically creating pollution, metastasizing a carcinogenic environment—

epitomized in the ever-expanding cities of the dying—and by the sentient weapons of modern invasion. The creators of artificial death belong to the same funereal fraternity as the various male supermothers—creators of artificial life and manipulators of existing life." Vivica Marigold is on a *facha* rant tangent, trying to ratchet the gadgets, and pointing at the sky.

It could be that I simply stand amidst all the smoking noise and observe as the guerillas take over the station. The Open Heart Surgery gang is gathering at the Drop Shadow Inn to confabulate. The entire J-Loop is already here, her various shes popping up in unexpected places.

"I thought you were in prison!" Gwenny exclaims as J-Loop momentarily cheshires a Heisenberg next to the figurine of a peach.

Everybody's talking from different directions, about total war, deals in East Asia and Europa, the new roachmeat patty Drive-by Burgers is currently test marketing, cachinating to the decibilly beat. Noggin grabs the mike and tom-cats something about pure sex, "waking up the neighborhood," he's such a braggart, the chaotic knots and blends the erotic make, and like speech, one horse-frightened syllable at a time. *The tongue follows the body.* Advertising tells us we are stupid but can be redeemed, made over and bright. Mental health is promoted because the aliens have made human culture a chronic disease. *These wounds stupend us.* Stupidity isn't just psychological or physiological theory, but is as real as shelling the ghetto: if we don't get the drift, we'll be argon fucks, and deserve to disappear up the sux.

Most of the rest of the crowd is busy J-Loop spotting, as there are reports her Janis Joplin incarnation materialized for a few seconds some time ago. *Where the hell is my body?*

Cauldron Salinger is silently and steadily sipping bourbon at the dark side of the bar. *I can hear you just fine. Now calm down; I'm busy.*

Because of their philia for illocatability, the gang's where-abouts are kept a secret. So secret, the gangsters themselves don't know where they are, and the venue itself is often an invisible college. The Open Mike gang writhes in the night, unseen, the uninvited of Oneirica, panthers padding on the pavement. The air is warm, close, smoky in their wake.

I watch Cauldron build pagodas with his shot glasses, but nobody will meet my eyes. It's as if I weren't here, or am hermetically sealed, but sometimes when I'm in the thick of things, I can't see the fog in front of my face, because a hailstone or a strangler has just knocked me unconscious.

◦ ◦ ◦

Gang-member J-Loop, especially, celebrates Storiella's initiation. She's a little Mayan in this respect; she lives with the dead all around her. Indefatigable on the forking road of karma, J-Loop always helixes back 'round where she started: reborn, rebooted, rebhodied, dharma tall. Curiously, her previous incarnations don't completely vacate the premises upon death. The deceased Janices, Juliannes, and Jaquilles aren't necessarily entirely present, just a flash of spirit here, a curve of breast over there, a rhyme of laughter circling. They follow the current J-woman around in a soulful cloud, hovering osmotically about her body. A thousand and one incarnations, women, with a few Judes thrown in, genetic memory given ghostly form, causing the lips of those who are asleep to speak.

◦ ◦ ◦

Deep in the woods, looking for their strayed particle charge, the gangsters encounter two axes, *signifiance* and *subjectification*. Signifiance is never without a white wall upon which it inscribes its signs and redundancies.

Subjectification is never without a black hole into which it lobs its consciousness, passion, and differences. Since operators are standing by, it should come as no surprise that a very special mechanism is situated at the axes' intersection. Oddly enough, it is a face in the television.

A broad face with white cheeks, a chalk face with eyes as cut-out black holes. The face is not an envelope exterior to the person who speaks, thinks, or feels. The form of the signifier will remain indeterminate if the subscribing viewer does not use the face of the speaker to guide her choices. Faces are not basically individual; they define zones of prepositional development, delimit a field that neutralizes in advance any expressions or connections unamenable to the appropriate significations. *Tune up and turn in.*

Assemblages are already different from prepositional zones. They are created in Cthonia, but operate in constituencies where zones become dismembered: they begin by extracting a *territory* from the zones. *Wolves howling; bonobos chimpering.* The assemblage's territoriality (content and expression included) is only a first aspect: another aspect is constituted by *lines of invasion* that cut across and carry the assemblage away, *stealing your face.*

"With his public masturbation, Diogenes committed a shamelessness by means of which he set himself in opposition to the political training mandatory in all zones." It's Tesana, the philosophy stripper. "It was a frontal attack on the nuclear politics of the family, the core of all conservatism, a joke on moose and squirrel. Because, as tradition ashamedly irradiates, he sang his wedding song with his own hands, he was not subject to the compulsion to get married to satisfy his sexual needs." Tes is pushing the crowd, several incarnations of J looping beside and behind her, a kind of plasmatic backup group. "I sense a manic finger fucking everybody into a perpetual orgasm of yay-saying, as if the sweeping away of denial were the true fruit of desire, but nobody wants to admit they're lying." *Cogito, ergo boom.*

"Diogenes taught masturbation by practical example, as cultural progress, mind you, not as regression to the animalistic. According to the wise woman, we should let the animal live, insofar as it is a condition of the human. The magical masturbator—if only we could drive away hunger by rubbing the belly—breaks through the conservative sexual economy without vital losses. Sexual independence remains one of the most important conditions of emancipation."

No doubting Tesana's independence; I can scent her fervid green from here.

To know the aliens is to begin to be free of them. They are unseen the same way we are in the mirror, too obvious to mention. Although it seems that whenever I've mentioned such things I've been slapped down with the insanity clause of unknowing. There's a lap around here somewhere. Or am I already dead, transient on a nine-lives guest visa? I remember I have no thumbs, and panic sets in.

∘ ∘ ∘

"Besides this intellectual trouble, she suffered from moral maladies of a similar sort. She had always taken for truth any assertion that sounded impressive and seemed to suit her ideas of right and wrong. She was shocked to the limit by our principles and conduct. Was she dreaming? Were we really living, loving and laughing, healthy and happy, when, by all rules, we ought to be shrieking with agony in the madhouse, the gaol or the lock hospital?"

Gwenny Spaghetti taps the mike, "tes tube tree core," checking to see if it's really on.

"The Oneirican government is a very precarious institution. Certain highly placed individuals within that government have possessed the knowledge of antigravity since the turn of the penultimate century. They even put this into effect in a battleship which was fully loaded with armaments and people. Its belly hung with generators that created a magnetic force, that created the vacuum, that created zero-degree temperature, that would allow it to raise the vibratory rate of the whole ship and the crew, transporting them to another place and time." Gwenny pauses to think for a moment, and then concludes aposiopetically, "And if I ever catch the bastards who took my Molly I'll—" punching the air above her head as if trying to fend off a fire descending from on high. Could our very grain have an infection? Are we on St. Tony's fire, crosses arcing in the air?

All over the world creatures blink. *Leap*: this is a matter of oil, lubrication. Friction is life, homeopathically, because oil begins with organic body death, and the oil distilled is the cure for friction. Necrogenesis, in some lost language, for I am a barbarian here. Before Babylon was dust the magus Zoroaster, my dead child, met his own image walking in the garden. Weep, sweet Enthymeme, for your sister Sophia is slipping away.

Invasion of consciousness, balkanization of states, schizophrenic's journal, fragmentary loopholes in a time-traveler's freshly laundered hay? Meaning is medial—like the ether—an ocean crashing full of bath salts, tumbling all the parts together.

∘ ∘ ∘

I look up from Cauldron's lap, startled by a familiar voice—by God's foreskin, it's Alaric the Astralgoth, foaming without aid of microphone, and unless my ears and whiskers are mistaken, projecting very well.

"If we wish for our lives we should diligently take the great medicines," Alaric booms as the voices quiet and things lurch back to Earth. "If we desire to communicate with the aliens we should drink solutions of metal and practice the multiplication of our psyches. By multiplying your psyche you will be able to see the ka soul and the ba soul within your body. You will be able to enter the presence of the aliens in their heaven, and the deities of the Earth, as well as have the spirits of the mountains and the rivers at your service."

I have no idea what the red-headed Goth is on about. Over on Tabasco Row they're smiling politely at their eggs. His tall handsomeness really is foaming at the mouth. He's looking a little fuzzy around the edges. He's not foaming, there goes his head. Alaric's getting the sux. *Thuck-poof*, he's gone, and I'm a plutogray puffball diving for safety beneath the bar. But that's it—the evacuation's just for Alaric. All's clear on the Western front.

"I never did trust that sacking bastard, but I doubt *that* was in his contract," Salinger says.

Still trembling and mewling like a kitten, I leap back into Cauldron's lap. His scrytch is drunkenly reassuring.

○ ○ ○

"Strictly directed reflection must be achieved with the cooperation of consciousness. Be warned that preconscious mental processes following laws of their own will not be tolerated."

AnonoBot threatens to garble a milling semi-circle of primate faces. It isn't like the rebusoid acquittal spits up anything unknown, the digitized sequence of a dark commander. There are no words to describe such an alien psychology in any known Diagnostic Standard Manual. Whatever mechanics are involved, it seems certain that the basis of implanted imagery lies in the actual structure of or processes within the human memory hologram, at the optical, the cellular, and the electrical levels. These can underlie more complex imagery, in the same manner that the stochastic dot array of a newspaper can carry photographic images.

A minor earthquake rattles some cages, whirs some nerves, and sends debris flying from the war-torn Hyatt's walls. No smoking. Dry flat. Stay tuned.

"Tickets, please!" says a guard, sticking his head through a window. In a moment all the gangsters are holding out tickets: each about the same size as a person, the tickets seem to fill the room.

"Security?" asks Beamish Boy, with a heavy bacon back-up waiting in the doughnut shop. I mink through the crowd looking for a better angle.

"No problem." Still can't see. Exilism is second state to these gangsters; they toy with the robots like mice. "Together we can find a way. We'll all pull together as a team." Thinking is a chorus.

We must gather for a picnic up on Rose Mountain and eat pot brownies and strawberry soup. If this is Tuesday, this transmission is live from the Dreamland test site.

"Really? How fast do we need to go?"

"You're breaking up!" *With me?*

"Just be cool," the schizochronometer instructs, glinting with sapphire rays. "There's a lemon-drop-headed alien standing in your ear." These gangsters can throw quite a scene, an Area 51 of the mind, always on the move, cutting the rug so as to leave no traces.

Without too much rudeness, Beamish Boy pushes aside the crowd for the Divinity of Oakland. There is a lot of ambiguously playful rowdiness, jallopying for position, and juxtaposing in time with the slow blue strobe. The smoke alone is worth a thousand shekels a puff.

The divine Calypso Agotime leads us past dusty cement factories for the Telesterion just now crystallizing on the horizon. We walk this way, mystai-eyed processors on the road to the epochalypse, cups in hand, smoking mint.

Von Hokhmah's psychic mansion has an atrium. I have the oddest feeling I'm back in my own body—home is where we hang our holograms. *Lover's lure.* We variously motivate through the atrium, which also houses avians, trees of many climes beseeched by twining vines, and a 200-foot-tall spiral staircase down through the middle of it all, which we now descend in a more or less gangsterly fashion.

On Von's south forty the Telesterion has almost completely crystallized, although how this could happen is a complete Greek mystery to me. Beamish Boy shoos the SPCK suiters in after, before, and between the actual entrance of the scientists from Berkeley. Auraless, I suspect they're Necks.

"Not to worry about spies," Agotime tells the new non-leader of the Ludic Sisters of Duality. "The roses are rigged with nanomikes."

Mildred Adorno, the untitled document, snorts. She may have a leak. Or she could be doing sound tonight.

"We're all spies," Adorno adumbrates.

I hear, but cannot speak.

The Telesterion is ready for us.

"Entrez hoo-doo dare, two the suite."

We arc in pairs 'cross the bright cuneiformed threshold and its tall scanning orifices, each personally greeted and cheek-kissed by Misty LeGog, the crux of the apostrophe cheesecake biscuit herself, the woman with the key to everyone's pheromone receptors, the one with whom we must all sleep in order to eat, trickster angel twins cohabitating a single olive female's body. *The twain shall meet.*

"Welcome to Eleusis," she invokes with a drop on every tongue.

I elude her? From what illusion comes this? And why is a goddess talking to a cat? Didn't somebody once tell me to expect sudden changes?

Into the marvel of the anarchist Iktinos, the Telesterion hall is carved entirely of granite, three floors, glass-racked igneous bars scattered, rock seats and cubbies arrayed in casual deliberateness, set and setting, three staircases up the back wall to the aerie suspended atop a column mushrooming out of the center of the hall. I wander toward one of the bars, minding millers' feet, seeking a snack.

∘ ∘ ∘

Armamentia comes over to the bar, grinning at deliquent Cody like a gangster. Cody smiles back, hanging eye contact like a glider. There are no physical colloquialisms when it comes to liquids. The people of the high desert say, *You either got it, or you don't.* Weak for water. Armamentia has snapping turtles at her feet, a signal for the mystery to begin to unfold. *A pale surge splintering on the strand of night,* purpling the claviceps and glands of the neck.

Madonna Curie rattles off the names and numbers of all the radioisotopes, and wins ten shekels on a bet from Cauldron Salinger, who pays up reluctantly, like granite on the move. Amanuensis Einstein shrugs proudly, a nimbus menacing o'er the greensward, puffs his bowl of whiskey crystal, his eyes far off, softly playing over the vid screen. If it walks like a duck I smell a fish.

I thought I was on a mission from Aquaknowledge to find my lover and drive out the invaders, but the Red King on the Mothership is wrenching things around. *You are engaged in a violet conspiracy.*

Dirty Breather!

Turn the fucken TV off.

You breathed first.

But what it is, I'm standing in a boy.

∘ ∘ ∘

I give Armamentia a kiss on the lips. She palms my cheek.

"It's so good to see you again!" I say. Voice works, I feel something else working too.

"So, you remember?" she asks, genuinely amazed.

"Tia Bila, how could I ever forget you? Have I ever misrepresented you? Thanks for not having me killed." The cat rubs against my legs, murmuring something I can't quite hear.

"Well, I thought you'd been pulled up the sux. Then Top Quark told me you were back—but from where?"

"I'm not sure. How long was I gone?"

All you have to do, Tia thinks, *is turn off the televisions.*

"Shut down the aquariums," I remind her.

"Tear up the magazines," says the cat.

"I saw you last month, remember?" She looks at me oddly. "At the Gazebo Go—" I start to feel a little shaky. Have I tripped over a ley line? Am I falling, shrinking, swelling toward the future?

"You must remember, these aliens want to suck us up. Mercenaries and photographers shoot first." Echoing; I can't place the voice. My tour guide seems unreliable. I may be ricocheting, four on the floor. "You roll over and beg," Crissi yells from behind the mike, like a marble flicked by a tricktser's thumb across a circle of asteroids. Memories are legion; truth is debonair; the telepathic countermeasures are beginning to nuke out the jams. Atom voice, the machine crashes and human interpretation and puzzle boxing must get to monkey wrenching. We teach the machine by learning to anticipate the needs of its cybernetic scanning orifices. But to scan, we must *meld*, our votive script lost to human sortie, the final delivery of an avant-mailmerge gestalt. So we *are* the homeless scum, *sorrowing eagles*; that's what all of this proves. Divining Metatron flagellates, we aid the aliens, not the Earth.

There *are* potassium-starved aliens out there, with suxual energy devices bought on sale at Target maybe aimed at this city. Chances are we'll only know where those weapons are at the instant of our vaporization—if we're lucky, crazy, or otherwise blessed. The UFO's power is in its drawing off of attention. But every animal heeds its sense of danger or eventually is extinguished in the roar of the night. The UFO is a semiotic laser pulse of clear-in-the-dark alarm. We only need briefly consider the thought—*alien*—to sense the flashing alert, the amnesial tentacles wrapping around our neocortexes.

"Jagged lightning blitzes his temple," spits a tenor from behind the mike. Just testing the sound?

∘ ∘ ∘

"The schematic nuptials, the pits of cyanide molecules, the tapeworms of technology's constricting parameters, these things and more in the next twenty hours will change your underwear. You think nylon is smart, knows when to hug, knows when to snug? Over here in Ward B they're already pulling down your nanopanties. And who is manu-facturing this intimate, intelligent garment? Infinite Star Systems, you got it." Margarine Not Butter is at the mike, or maybe it's Gwenny Spaghetti; hard to tell the sequels apart from this distance with all the smoke.

"Television is the only voice remaining in the global pil-lage. It has infiltrated every area of culture, of conscious-ness. That's why the market was freed, the forces of capi-tal unleashed. Religion, the State, all culture have been conquered, sacked for rhetorical treasure, and left in the various temples lobotomized, enslaved, entrained with the TV's alien hum." The crowd is getting jittery. *Everybody knows.* A few people leave. It's definitely Gwenny.

"Headless, and though we don't like the feeling, we are, gulp by toxic gulp, condemned to believe in civilization as if it were gravity or air. And here we are, friends, roam-ers, country persons, milling on the margins, trying not to get wet. It's not going to go away. We're going to have to fight. We're going to have to fight the sux."

○ ○ ○

I sense there are telepathic creatures lurking in the dark of the moon, that consciousness may be some sort of self-illuminating foam, that mutability and adaptability are energies radiating with the beat of the big magma. *Death deserves to come as a surprise*. Venus on the Half Dome, gyring on the gimbled waves, life's a game of pick-up-sticks, a crap shoot in a hurricane. Reconcatenated, the demon Strable is linguistic proof of human agency and control over nature. A demon who goes *thuck-poof* every time that control is shown up as a lie, a power trip, by an earth-quake or an alien invasion. A demon who, however, al-ways reasserts itself as soon as the shaking stops. A de-mon who, in the split between nature and perceived real-ity, gives us a narrative allowing us to retrieve memories and rebuild roads.

I could be spilling my guts to the Necks in a reuptake-inhibited block outage, but I can't see who's talking. I seem to be experiencing technical difficulties. No, I'm turning to face southeast, antennæ at attention. I'm getting KOH on the skip. Do I even have ears at the moment? I don't feel quite myself; I may not be home right now.

And that's when I see him, see me, my body out in the world looking for someone, divided observer, cause of bifur-cation an implant looking curiously like a late-night TV screen the size of a fingernail, damaging the core-textual synapses, symptomatically displaying as forgetfulness and enhanced telepathic ability, leaving me stranded and un-differentiated, ricocheting off one consciousness to the next.

I didn't die. I woke up.

○ ○ ○

Tesana comes up to the mike. Tongued limes, iso'd. Tabasco, please.

"I wonder if an object too dense to release light is any *purer* for the experience. Does it rank as a sort of Everyobject? Are catatonic people setting a standard for the rest of us? Is the electromagnetic spectrum a model for the perceptual limitations implicit in any nonblind species of life? And other related questions."

I have no idea where I am but I can't believe Tesana remembers that rocky passage. Whoever's eyes these are unfocus, roll, and I'm—

"Where flows the semiotic fluid, so consciousness washes with it. With consciousness moves all action and response. The semiotic flood is directed by the topography of prepositions: through, under, over, by. There is only motion; time is swept away. It is one thing to do something *for* but palpably more sinister to do something *to* the human race.

"The aliens do not exclusively or even primarily consist of fangs and claws. They are a vast network of tentacles moving by land as well as by sea. These tentacles are merchant caravans which transport commodities and medial entrainment by horses and camels, or in the holds of ships. Eventually, discord reaches the ancient metropolis of Cern Francisco." *Kismet operatically harrowing.* "Two parties form, a Worm Party and an Octopus Party. The authoritarians in the Worm Party know that an empire needs a large concentration of military power to keep from dismembering. The merchants in the Octopus Party know that wealth comes from freely moving tentacles, and that a large military concentration would eat up the resources of the empire. The merchants know that the tentacles are not free human beings but bits of armor, parts of the polis, splinters which, like arrows, serve their purpose only when they're loosed."

There are no sad violins waiting for the final amnesia, the one that will erase an entire life. *Kali—over here!*

"The gangsters will try, but not completely protect us from a ravaging marauder on a mission of greed."

It was all an axle dent; the Mothership never meant to come here. The warp engines were al dente in the stoics of timelines misspoken and twisted, the only edible consciousnesses for light-decades a globelet teeming with pungent primates, unruly but sustaining. AnonoBot rolls by, silent as a plague. A bomb explodes an ocean surrounding Kava Kava. Tonight's *prix fixe*: boiled filet of cathode ray, served with a plasma of Antonioni and cheese. Somewhere far off a telephone softly rings? Pauseways vertigoing toward future's rearing.

○ ○ ○

Reef knows a woman made of stone. Her curves are so finely chiseled that light is guided right through her, barely bending when she moves. The air shimmers, and if it's quiet enough, he can hear her footsteps through the grass, but these are her only signs. Otherwise she is completely invisible, a living statue carved from a single crystal of pure leonardolite.

Reef met her when she touched him one night. He was wanting the succor of the sound of the sea so dragged his sleeping bag down to a copse of trees on the beach. Sacked, he stared at the stars, puzzling and premonitory, until he finally drifted into a light sleep.

She tapped his cheek.

He opened his eyes and looked around. Nothing? Just a minor brain spasm, he concluded, and closed his eyes again.

She laid her hand on his cheek, and kept it there.

He grasped the hand, gasping at how cool and smooth it was. She pulled her hand away easily, stronger than water, no weeping woman, yet wary, perhaps remembering.

"Who's there?" Reef whispered, afraid that he'd finally

snapped from island fever.

She couldn't answer, can never speak her name, but placed her hands gently on his chest. He put his two hands on top of hers, and tried to relax. It wasn't easy: his eyes kept scanning, desperately, brain searching for even a single photon of starlight reflected by the woman's body. But there was not one.

They stayed like that the rest of the night. Occasionally he would dare to stroke her wrist, and be amazed, as if by a hallucination. Her skin had the texture of stone so finely polished it was as if it didn't exist at all, something so frictionless the rest of the world barely notices a ripple as she passes by.

◦ ◦ ◦

A Blancámoor princess draws her sword and cleaves the knot of consciousness. She hurriedly rewires the remote. Her cat is a cross between an owl and a bear. An overabundance of facts blows out of control, ripping through our sails. Massive population expeditions flee before the saucers that come flying out of cracks in the Earth. An entire TV nation and there's nothing on. A human woman sits weaving point in a pattern of light taught her by Grandmother Spider. *You are coming through in code.*

"Of all the ways the sunflower has of loving the light, regret is the most beautiful shadow on the sundial. Crossbones, crossword puzzles, volumes and volumes of ignorance and knowledge. Where is one to begin? The fish is born from a thorn, the monkey from a walnut. The shadow of Christopher Columbus itself turns on Tierra del Fuego: crazy love is no more difficult than the egg."

Judy Thursday is pitching woo, but her voice is drowning. Someone else comes foaming to the microphone.

"Pythagoras charged his disciples not to eat brain or heart. That is, they should not consume the brain with empty thoughts, nor burn out the heart with excessive cares. If all things happen by chance, they labor in vain who presume to control completely, and to manage by fixed principles of reasoning, affairs that in countless ways happen beyond reason. If all things come from fate, those who strive to avoid what is an unavoidable necessity fall more heavily into fate, for to it they are adding their own labor." It's Arabesque, reading from the catechisms, as if children we had become, with lasagna in our hair.

"And another thing—are you listening to me?" *Keening, that note was....*

∘ ∘ ∘

"The primary order of the world can be re-established."

The Open Mike crowd is starting to break out in all directions. I'm back among the living?

Esmeralda, testing her wings, with Margarine Not Butter on tabla, is indulging her entheophasia. "Through a mutual desire for the fusion of our bodies and souls, we will fulfill the intercepted message." Her implant looks swollen. "Make love as a way of combatting the world's confusion, of restoring desire to its rightful and essential place, and of feeling the generative fire from above which is also blood, milk, and semen."

I wend along in search of kibble.

Bernard Slackercode and Uncle Lucifer are negotiating a treaty at the bar. "A pint of Kompound d'Harmaline," a desire unbroken, "from the Cantabrian Mountains." *Qué pasó? KOH sings of me?* At last minute's open mike they had telekinetically materialized a Baby loRad on top of the pool table in the back room. The boys can get a little tweaky when they've had their Bushmills.

"Separation, division, and scattering are specifically terrestrial signs of alienation, but these are just illusion. They are the mirages of another world as yet uncreated, unengendered, although it exists in a latent state in the hill country beyond Rose Mountain, and we must ask our-

selves whether it is perhaps the appointed task of the gangsters to bring it into being, to materialize the Wooden World
by awakening the total consciousness of humankind, by
fleeing from the mirage and stepping through the illusory
looking-glass which is at once our earth and our sky."

I'm rounding on a faerie's wheel.

"Blood is transformed into wine; ruthless slaughter and
the martyr's death are transformed into a merry banquet;
the stake becomes a hearth. Bloodshed, dismemberment,
burning, death, beatings, blows, curses, and abuses—all
these elements are steeped in carnival, a time out of time
which kills and gives birth, which juvenesces and allows
nothing old to be perpetuated, never ceases to generate
the new and the neotenous."

I feel as if I am somehow invisible.

"Clouds on the horizon that can bring a devastating
storm. An image which forms a reality where nothing
oppresses but the turbulent engines of the atmosphere.
Orgone lurches and steams, nimbus and hail, rushing up
into thunderheads and running down along long valleys
as a calm breath of annealing air. It all *depends*. Old saying: A butterfly's wingbeat in Shanghai can brew a tem-
pest in a teacup in Djakarta. On you. Imagine, then, that
this argument is a dance. And remember when you're
putting your body back together, that clouds carry a message from the future of initial conditions. A message from
an alien in a pixilated fish tank, oozing along on your living room floor."

What is this microphone doing here?

∘ ∘ ∘

The Mixter of Alterity for this evening's Open Mike irruption, Delmar Erwington, hooters, "Guarded from
within, so seemed he entering his shadow." All kinds of
fictional assumptions occur, are traded on the mock exchange where bones are measured. Nairbula shakes his

head, prophetically sighs. Wolfgang Amadeus Muskrat sacks the microphone with a satanic blast from his barium saxophone. The gangsters stomp their bass feet, from the Western Lands to Floating Manhattan, setting up a resonance fit to break the glass. Stink, and to Jésus Crypto-Power over-pumping nominalism, the babble comes in with all its strength, all its speak.

When you're out on parole rhythm funks a body, and what is said is said is said by any other sane, *you rose me?*

○ ○ ○

J-Loop sees Nairbula get pulled up the sux. First the ancient astronomer's caftan flutters and starts to billow and his baby-fine long white hair is tugged straight up. For a moment he seems to blur and stretch, but then he's gone, disappearing with an implosive pop. *Don't forget to breathe.*

A *coup d'état* is an attempt to change the government by a short sharp shock to the machinery of administration. Under the proper conditions, a comparatively small number of determined humans can capture the state at low cost. The possibility is very attractive to discontented spiritual minorities. *Memento mori.* Humans who could never hope to raise or equip armies for civil war, or who have no chance of calling forth or controlling the furies of revolution, may see in the *coup d'état* a fulcrum by which they can move the world. It has been done more than once with terrible effect.

"De Molay, thou art avenged!" *Flag aloft.*

"Duck, you suckers!" *Molotov.*

"I am going to throw you in the brig for this!" *Call them off.*

Mark Lakoff moves the chess pieces around the board. It's a code, a signal to the other human insurgents. The recusants piously cup their implants so the Necks won't notice their furtive behavior. On the Mothership, Alaric the Astralgoth imagines how humans remember, trading his knowledge for his life. In the artificial cleft beneath Styx Valley the collaborators don new clothes. Bureaucracy becomes a fugue with many variations.

My shot, brought to you in part by members like you, bombs away, mate the Red King in four. Nothing is weaker than water.

Down the hatch.

Gertrude Stein burps from garlic and pasta, passes the late-hour guests, climbs the spiral through the furling snow, and switches on the lighthouse beacon. The punk chick with the gray hair and the wandering eye jumps up to the open mike. "Remember," she reminds us, "the buck stops now where near you." *Nothing can go wrong*, her gaze seems to say. And so I lost my ignorance on the floor of the temple of funhouse mirrors, a pussy full of mint.

Tesana stops snoring, lies perfectly quiet for a moment, then sits bolt upright and says, "Was I dreaming?" A satellite hears her and relays the question to the Mothership. *Another day, another mind*—but who says that? Mathematician? Junkie? Alien? Mad woman? Or will the Future travel back in time and come kick my ass, call me a lying sack of shit as I'm lying in a Hilo gutter? *Face down in the mud, can't see...*

"You decide, then, you decide the fate of human fucking manatee, you decide and just leave me alone." *A golgatha of depression...*

"And it is exactly this wall of terror we must ascend." *A resurrection of creation.*

We are breathing the invisible. Vicious circles break thorugh the watery glass, daisy-chaining in soulful spirals. A preternatural certainty pervades the gangsters. We've seen the cut and know the score. The initiation continues harum-skarum, everybody snake dancing past the microphone, invoking the golem with a line or two each. The corpse takes exquisite form in the air above us, and the roof of the Telesterion is swept away. Judy Thursday couples with a lone stranger, and down there rains a flood of rose petals upon the recusants.

The gangsters back themselves up on a harmonium wind gifted at birth with Aqua-knowledge in the mountains of Bhutan, like Uncle Lucifer's crime reports read as a taunt at the regime, a wind from the righteously outraged lungs of the world that blows a spark into the hair of Abernathy Alhambra McDruther, follicle-singeing a strand from his pate, hurricaning it through the inner workings of Anonymous Robot's positronic brain, turning it into a wind chime which plays a chord that catches the ear of Thelonious Monk, who sits down at the bar piano and composes "Epistolary," and Mildred Adorno, with Irwin Spellbottom producing, gets it all on tape while Madonna Curie, Amanuensis Einstein's hand on her ass, peers carefully through a magnifying glass, looking for isotopes like specks of dust mayhaps carried in by the breeze that suddenly stirs the room.

We all look up, amazed, around us only silence like a blinding light, as if every yesterday before this moment has been a lie lived by somnambulists, and everybody—from Arabesque up by the stage to Zebra Democritus off in the hinterlands of the pay phones, and the whole J-Loop between materializing randomly around the room as Scry watches bleary eyed through a telescope—now blinks, grins sheepishly, and stretches like a cat just up from a nap.

Euryale's Veil

SCRY IS TAPPING CRYPTIC SEARCH STRINGS into her lapcache, cross-referencing *The Thousand and One Voices*, seeking clues for a path, finding only St. Tony's fire. Denny is studying *The Hero with a Thousand Faces* on his micro-fiche reader. Margarine chords her lute, *kaliope our haven*, while Gwenny stands guard, facing southeast. I'm hunching my shoulders, checking for missing parts.

Ginja, cube rooting and learning fast, wields her malleable nemesis, now a shield of glass, fluid as spontaneous laughter and alluring as drops of blood to sharks. Ginja is dialing every number in the world, seeking connections to facilitate her own sort of movement. When all the ways of answering the phone have been tried, and when the surf finally calms on the beaming hot television beach, the stars will begin to slowly blink out.

I spread leaves for a reading, something I learned to do from a lesbian at Bryn Mawr. The leaves say I should have remembered and done what I forgot and didn't. It's hard to look on the past and know I could have finessed something to change what was then still the future. *When once we did descry—*

Which is precisely what they want us to believe. The outlines of the invasion are obscured by a hurricane of hypergnosic details. I may be doing exactly what Aquaknowledge wants me to do—*the immortal man who cannot die.*

"Dense, fast memory is expensive," Ginja says. She who shrinks to nano size. She who by Scry's imagining lets us slip from ignorance, soft goddess tissue of self-machinating inscription. *I hope I can remember.*

"Or had forgotten about," Reef mutters, *not Kansas at all*, seeing the virus code butterfly out of the e-mail from Scry, *I'm sounding in the channel's tumbling tide.* The code begins to precipitate avatartrates, and then Ginja appears, Scry having correctly gamboled in the chaos waves that Reef wouldn't just switch off the cache when the virus started installing herself. *Curioser and curioser.*

"We will fix their wagons," Ginja says, synching up her face. "We will put our ducks in a row. Ah, here we go. Hi, Reef, I'm boot-strapping myself into existence on your system—hope you don't mind if I hang for a while. I'm Scry's latest software, Ginja." She explodes her head into a pixel-perfect waterfall of paisleys. "I've really only got one purpose in artificial life." *Invisible Khidr, guide of Moses.*

"What's that?" Reef is feeling heavily boggled, trapped in his body, like the war is getting maybe a little too close.

"To transmit a biosemiotic navigational signal into outer space."

"How can I help?" Reef ever grows, *kelp, otters; above an airy eagle hovering in the current.*

"I need a balloon in which to transmigrate the sux in order to target the signal."

"And I know a pirate with a balloon."

"Yes. And I'll help you look for Silas Proton on the way." She already is, simultaneous parallelisms.

Reef nods, glacial warming in the mountains of his heart, and telegraphs Gelmanov, *Get yr ass good guy hover here.*

○ ○ ○

Scry is darning a sock. "Getting ready for a big hike," she claims of the future, and tells us what we're going to do.

"We'll slide down those tunnels there, hare tail it down these corridors here, and when we find the collaborationists' hive, we'll loRad the bastards."

Denny is intently twisting a dreadlock, staring unfocused at the polyphony of photocopies that skins the floor in patterns that explode all Freytagian principles of architecture.

The psychographic map of Styx Valley is spread out in front of us, a composite of gothic blueprints and stolen NSA drug-test reports cobbled together by the Matrix librarian, or an Atlantean refugee of her acquaintance, or maybe some bored grunge working graveyard at a copy shop. I don't think any one of us really knows what we're looking at, but when two or more gather?

"So we're just making this up?" I ask.

"Exactly," Scry says. "All sorts of free-thinking anarchists and independents will be routing and scheming for us, opaquely milking serendipity. We'll have to check chances and clues carefully, but with intuitive abandon, because this is all going to happen very fast."

"Kind of an uncarved block type of thing, huh?" Denny asks.

Scry laughs like a song bird, and pulling her thread through says, "I'd applaud your intuition, but I don't even have one hand free."

∘ ∘ ∘

Kundalini, tantra, scarification, chanting until consciousness is churning, fasting, thirsting, purification, exposure. Sensations of weightlessness, macroscopia, depersonalization, and alteration or loss of time perception are normally experienced. *Lie with me in the shallow salty sea.*

Mind control is often conceived as somehow manipulating language, thought, seizing control of the interior engine driving the call and response of communication. It's not that at all. It's bats fleeing a cave suddenly discovered hollow with illumination descending.

Pass me the eye. Have you got your wallet and keys? *And on my turban, wings to hurry me to you.* Are we going someplace dangerous?

The unrequited love that does indeed reply in kind. *One molecule in a trillion.* The predilection of science is to bring the unseen into view. It's really a conspiracy—despite ourselves—to manipulate the secret vocabulary of our bodies. *We all breathe the same air.* There are many trails, everything is in proximity, we want the big magma. I have finally perceived a message from KOH. *Proliferate, my love.*

"Comma on," I stutter nervosively at the others. "Let's get the fux out of here." The Pyramid of Chopin preludes before us, and we'll get no refund if it rains too soon. *You've been gorgon for far too long.*

⚬ ⚬ ⚬

Aquaknowledge holds in a breath that is thought transfixed; she can metamorphose desire and mercy and the thousand other splinters that the eye can't blink. Out for a walk in the Wooden World she communicates like a bird drinks dew, the transmutation of the very air, the webbing works and play of minds everywhere. She is the mother of the spirit that curls like a horse unwinding on a long run, the two-gathered thing that stiffens against the soft, erecting walls against the flood of catastrophe natural or alien. She is a delta where the river meets the sea. She is the hidden center, to embrace and caressed by be. God pinions us, an alien pin jabs us to a collection board, but Aquaknowledge dissolves all that by chanting *barbar* and dancing with her hips.

⚬ ⚬ ⚬

As children, Armamentia Bila and I grew up together for a few years. We were precocious sweethearts, but eventually our wandering tribes moved apart. *Traveling changes to return.* Many years later, I looked for and found her living in a border town. We got back together, and married. We never spoke of our childhood. It was as if it had never taken place, or an unbridgable chasm had grown between the present and the past. *We aren't children any longer,* she said the one time I mentioned our story, *and have put away childish things.* I don't remember the initiation, *embarking through a revolving door.*

Armamentia was the queen of denial, a drunkard's dream, but I couldn't drink like that—too weak, can't swim. Cool, mellow, no—hooded and glum, surly and raging. I drank like alcohol was Christ's blood and I couldn't get enough of the stuff that coursed through the veins of the world. When I finally stopped drinking, Armamentia discovered I was boring, no longer polymorpheus's fire descending from above, and left in a huff.

I suddenly realize I can remember yesterday perfectly and it doesn't add up; time's been stolen by the free-market mind mongers. I'm just another day older, nothing so awful. The dissociation is definitely down, focus is good. Olduvai jaw, the alveolar holes stand in stark relief, crenelations of a wall that will either humble to dust or pave the Earth entirely. *Toothache.* Lateral tracking systems functioning normally. So why am I lying flat on my back in the sand? *The family changes to great power.*

Armamentia had a daughter from the days before she got on the bus. The child's name was Samantha. Samantha was well into her months when I met her, 18 or 20. Her mother's breasts were still swollen with milk for her. Ludic and charming, Samantha could wiggle her nose and make things disappear. For instance, a pair of my underwear which her mother found obstreperously square.

Some coincidence—this was due to Aquaknowledge, not the washing machine's hunger for salty yarn, when

one fine summer's eve Tia Bila drugged me up and dragged
me out to hear Hermetic Definition. Did I ever meet such
a motley crew and over the coals walk so entrancingly? I
should try to sit up. *Perseverance furthers.*

The violet crumbles are falling again. I wish I knew
what causes them. *It's the alchemical smelling salts.* They're
like dried foam, suddenly filling the air with purple
sparkles, as if precipitating out of some electrolytic solution. I'm not the only one who sees the fall. The cat lifts
her head from her paws and stares. And then they're gone
again, just as quickly. *No rain in the western lands.* The
others are already over the hill, catching some shade.

By weight, the brain is approximately one percent inor-
ganic salts. Potassium ions play a significant part in the
salting of the brain, acting as catalysts in the stimulation
of interpsychic perception, and play a key role in the pro-
duction of emotion, sluicing the paths to memory with
brine. When this part of the brain's chemistry is altered,
spontaneous laughter or crying may occur.

Pea brain, cesium me, clicking like a Geiger countering
a banshee. Radiation is the scream of the goddess. Things
fall apart, the mesons keep rolling along, concepts decom-
pose. Can I survive the stench as semiotic fungus slows
me to a dead crawl? Technology, like cities, is built on
ruins, but is obscured by a cognitive mist that scatters my
tentative thoughts. I've got sand in my mouth.

The gangsters tell me I love her, but will I in time ever?
I want to kiss you all over all over again. Erotic emotions
are caviar to the aliens. I shouldn't think of her, but must
or betray our jihad. There's no back to go or give up to.
Armamentia slips through the shamal, I feel buffeted by
the wind. I can almost smell the past, like the scent of an
unseen woman who has just walked by. *Everybody's talking at you*—whose hand pulls me up?—*will I see you again?*

The town is fog, and granite has decimated into pale

gluey sand the color of static. I walk out of the pale blue wonder, hear the sirens through the fog. Shame is the masthead of social conformity, the compass point where external sails are transformed into internal shibboleths, I hear every word they're saying. *Are you coming to collect me?*

○ ○ ○

"I have always wondered about sexuality, and it is suspicious to assign gender on the basis of genitals, as if imgination were so frail." Gwenny Spaghetti, at once hard boiled and flexible, sits thumb-rocketing pebbles across a swiftly tilting planet.

"We lack a physiology of grammar, we don't use the proper words. Who enters the gates of ecstasy, who climbs the pillar of pride? These are daimonic emotional questions, like leather or lace, like identity itself. Paracelsian medicine turned to the patient and tried to make accute differential perceptions. There is no unified field theory; everything is mirrors and steam. We should paint glissando desire all over gender but instead dwell upon it unto death, like a bone or a country. The leavening question is always the one of difference, leaving the problem open as a door by which the soul may enter."

"I want some of what she's got," Denny and I say. *Jinx, you owe me a switch back.*

What tea kettles? Who whistles? What's up? I look and Orion's hunting, it's—*dzizt, piss and vinegar—incoming!*

Parabolistic memos signifying retribution carom around us, we duck and cover. Daggers of unconscionable intent snap us up like flashbacks through the synthetic carpeting. As the monitors implode on contact with the sudden event horizon, the gangsters' heads first stretch, then are souped into the implosion, an entire body quickly vaporizing in a trail before disappearing with a lip-sucking pop into the vacuum. *Hold on,* I distinctly hear KOH, *stay still,* but it's all over in a few seconds.

We are left standing, listless, staring, shocked, survivors clasping in a crystalline complex of the missiled metropolis, now tinged blue with the blood of comrades suxed but not forgotten. Multiples are missing. We murmur eulogies, taste death's fugue, but insist on, many mountains still to transit, a thousand seething cities, dangerous paths, infested with misdirection, full of holes, from the middle of the road out to the thin ice. Everywhere is the space of bodies, not just our own but the environment of trees and gutters and buildings and rocks, distance and the time it takes to cross, the time it takes sounding brass to echo. We can't go back to a past that is no longer, and the future shoots inexorably ahead, elusive as a shiver of recognition.

We grope forwards, toward a crawly-brawly sluggy sac of consciousness a-getten towards Birthmayhem and the creche of Her breast. The secret handshake is spit, which dissolves all sins in the palmistry. We remember the names of the days, but aren't always on the right one. A drowned sylph hallucinates no futures. *You've got to keep moving*, the changing lines she gives my face, *fire on the mountain does not linger*.

∘ ∘ ∘

Permeable is the night, a web of exchanging chaining molecules shaded from the sun by the gibbous moon. It is coolness, silence and absence which argue with the rays, and it is these that I call shade. Certain gangsters deliberate and take action, stockpiling the shade at night, and shovel it like mad on the irradiants of day, as if by some great barrier they can keep out the hordes. Others of us wander aimlessly, happy to be grim in the action of the moment, travelling solar, tided to a lunar perspective.

The streets of the world are like butter, guts churning, loins separating the cream from the chaff. Even through the pavement we can feel the magmic suck and thrust. I start building scale models with every eye I meet. The alien strategy of consciousness seeks the rays; when they start to ooze we put on stilts. And so the night becomes organized. *Commutas in the wilderness.* We press on, periodic as steam.

We seek an arc through the bull's horns. Appearing ignorant, we construct a contradiction. The bull is real; the arc is real. The state of passing-through is what never ends—and thus to some seems unreal? We record the past in the great dead languages of the future, mulching ourselves in like worms that feed on the sky. To abandon thinking in opposites is to swell consciousness. Such an expansion feels like a shaking of the foundations, because it means also dynamiting the belief that being can finally be accounted for in terms of simple abstract pairs held in mystical tension.

Lying is an abandoned contradiction, hallways of speech that bifurcate into simultaneous alternate universes not quite registering floorplan to floorplan. It is axiomatic that lies can come like swans or swarms of roaches, and in any of the 202 colors of the Tartaric alphabet. Having lived, I do not. I lie to subvert my lover's breath from the vacuum tube. It's the intentional cut in order to share blood. Blood and the memory of being wounded are our only proof of humanity, the things that save us from becoming what eats us.

Truth is not defined here, in the Western manner, by an inaccessible singularity: it is resumed here and there, and it runs from difference to difference, arranged in the great syntagmata of bodies. The laying on of hands is an absenting of pain, a silencing of demons, and a cooling of the rays. Bullshitting is theatre, and that's the only way we'll ever get down these streets.

○ ○ ○

Margarine Not Butter has been scouting ahead, and is

just returning. I climb out of my portable chemotherapy unit long enough to hear her report, which appears to be arranged in pieces across several acres of real estate. AnonoBot can really fly with those jetted heels; is that thing following us? *Contemplation: see and be seen.* The CEO of Infinite Star Systems calls a meeting in the hollow of Styx Valley. We all skulk on a ridgetop, listening in telepathically with headphone vine medicine.

"In a sense, we are in the same ethical and moral dilemma as the physicists in the days prior to the Floating Manhattan Project. Those of us who work out here in the field see a developing potential for total control of human emotional status. There is a lot of spanking going on, a lot of heavy criticism. A lot of enclosing in dark rooms. Welts are left. And why are the aliens so interested in cryptomnesia? Let me jog your memory. To study the effects of sixteen newly concocted biosemiotic warfare agents on humans—government off the books—including choking, blistering and vomiting agents, toxins, poison gas and incapacitating—"

"Network, we have control, though it may be intermittent. We have an aphasiac conglomeration of object-oriented news programming, and we think you ought to take a look at this footage."

"Agreed," Walter Spreadhike responds expediently. "Send Red Rover on over." But then the dish rotates; the channel changes.

May I tentatively outline a word aside? *Nazca lines describe cosmic urgasms.* We salve the insurgent in gratitude for her intelligence.

"Little do they know. Or maybe that's what they want us to think," Scry murmurs. *Do you think I can't hear you, Scry?* "I'm crossing my own path." *We are souls triangulating.* "This way," she sighs, pointing southeast. *The tyrant Anxiety.*

In the distance we hear roars, moans, cries of shrill laughter. The Open Mike gang is throwing a diversion. AnonoBot is in quite a scurry, and people, some with animal acts, are showing up from miles around.

"Let's do it again," cahoots Uncle Lucifer, licking her thighs, her globular clusters. "There is a limit to all things and this is nowhere close." *Is this really me?*

"Na strovya."

"I don't drink. I mean I was thinking. I was—"

"You were drifting."

"No, I think my connection with KOH is expanding," I say to Scry. *Shame changes to fortitude.* From bud to flower, and every place we went together. "The Necks have her on drugs, but she's resisting the seizure, arrows flying from her fortified walls."

∘ ∘ ∘

We're making up reasons, reasons to continue searching for one another or some other personal illusion of freedom, inventing imaginal universes that won't chafe our will to desire—based on little more than a millisecond's eye contact, the curve of cheek and brow in the dying light outside an outback espresso shack.

That's it, then; the will to desire undercuts every other foundation, and in our souls feels nothing at all to do with genes but everything to do with saying at night's end, "I was not alone."

We're hearing voices but we don't know where they're coming from; the sounds seem miles from anybody. Our burning breasts are full, yearning ignites and binds our horde. I finally know what Tia meant. Swan dive sea cruise, to see in life what we thought we only dreamed.

We smoke the shade at night, and I'd swear we're covering miles by day, swept along by the momentum of our unmasking, an ion storm motivating to the mountains.

∘ ∘ ∘

Denny stops dead in his tracks. I think I'm going to bump into him, my inertial dampers flailing, but I pass right through him. *Figures*, I think, but then can't remember what I was summing. I manage to stop and turn around.

"I just walked right through you," I point out to anybody who's interested.

"So noted in the log," Denny says, distracted. He's sniffing the breeze.

Scry is slowly walking in circles, her arms above her head, her fingers tapping the air.

"I'm definitely getting something here," Denny whispers.

"I'm picking it up, too." She turns and faces southeast. "It's your girlfriend's mnemon trail." Scry is suddenly standing rock still, expression bittersweet.

"KOH?" I ask urgently, ready to fire all phasers.

"The particle wave is holographic. I'm getting everything at once, the future and the past of the trail. Which ends in Styx Valley, I'm sorry to say."

"KOH is down in the Valley? But I've been so careful—"

"Not so fast," Scry cuts me off. "You're not entirely to blame. Things are a lot more complex than we realize. The aliens and the Necks have set this up, set *us* up, and they're luring us to the Valley. The aliens must be years ahead of us, as if they're looking at us behind them in a mirror. We'll have to unpredict ourselves in order to free KOH and blow up the command center." *Objects may appear larger, but Mary moved the rock.*

"But there's something you don't know. Denny, there's something I have to tell you. A while ago, I split up—"

Watch your step— The demon Strable throws down those who stand upright; he perverts the tongue and distorts the lips. Foam comes instead of words; we are filled with darkness: eyes open, yet our souls see not through them; and the miserable quiver convulsively. *Softly in a corner near by you, standing.*

The demon Strable leaps out from inside a boulder, grabs Denny and me by the scruffs and knocks our heads together, as if to force us to reunite according to some rain gage of normalcy. Our lion rages and our sulfur burns. Our saint is pecked by vultures, shot with arrows, burned at the stake.

Scry batters the demon's continuum with blows from an indoor-outdoor thermometer, reducing him to a point, which Denny brushes off his shoulder like a speck of dandruff or volcanic ash, a rain of original sin condensing in a word.

Weathering under a telepathic cloud, I feel like squalling, sourmash peat truck.

"That was close. We better keep moving," Scry says grimly.

○ ○ ○

And there, among the trees, I can see a minuscule man standing, waving at the camera of KOH. I have no idea when I got this picture, I think I've been carrying it for years. Perhaps she snapped it with her ankles gently bathing in the soothing South Sea. Everything that suddenly lights up, that draws my joy, that flares with beauty, each bush a god burning: this is the flammable face of the world, its phlogiston, its aureole of desire, enthymesis everywhere. Conflagration and coagulation occur together. I am indistinguishable from the objects of my desire, Scry, KOH, Denny, gangsters one and all. So warp and woof are expressed through time and space, and from a poverty of stimulus, an overabundance of meaning.

Aquaknowledge tries to acknowledge bloodstain and reason, emotion of sacrifice, heating remorse, hard-won smart streets. By Poe's walls a monkey grabs my arm, trickster sardonicus. *You can't take it seriously.* The painted

walls are slowly growing closer. I see the tension in the
dry, clenched throats, the tumorous implants, netizens
shunting off to another day of aquarial monotony, making memories for the Mothership, blind to our rolling thun-
derstorm circus of bedlam rovers, big massa confusa, ille-
gal tender is the night, every knot of thought for miles
around, skunking and throwing off scents both desperate
and calculated, pulp up the sux. Talking seems to do no
good, but talking is all there is, kiva our heretics. I thought
Denny was going to drive us? *There was something I was
spying—*

"My name is Nike."

"Pleasant how-do. Are those wings on your feet?"

"Yes, they're parrots."

"So, you too can fly? Are not locked to the ground?"

"Clear to Paris, Texas, if you like. These babies are the
wings of victory."

"Are there Huguenots in Paris?"

"Yes, but they're called Argonauts there, as the locals
have taken up some ancient Greek mannerisms."

"Like fucking each other in the ass?"

"No, that part's not new. Like taking some weird kind
of alkaloid in a crowded room, and then raving about in a
bus looking for mountains to move. Light's changed, I've
got to fly."

Don't listen to them. Something's tuning me, dishing me
up. *Listen to me.*

What if power is already in our hands? They can't hear
me. Is that a car alarm? How would we even know?—in
this day of disembodied intelligence, being poured from
molds most non-exemplary: from the none to the particular out of the general, the molds themselves force-injected
in a consentory. *No, you* must *listen to me.* Please stand by
while they declare me bankrupt and fit for jumping out a
financial-district window. Is what. Get a fucken clue. Buy

a loRad now, while I still can. *Stop—wait—*

This is who I am talking to, I know. *Take my fingers, I am yours, I can go where the body cannot.* It's easier to listen when you touch me.

—with my little eye. I was a kleptomaniac. I haven't had anything to steal in a long time. How long has Denny been driving? We used to stop at Whitewater for a beer. *Something that begins with K.* If we had any beer—there was none at Whitewater. *Kittens ogled hastily.* Just rocks, boulders really, lunar. *Sirch.* The landscape was brown with gray boulders everywhere. *Ekim.* And a rushing stream tearing through the barrens of the desert like a flood of relief. Who was there with me? Perhaps my brother Will— though I may not have recognized him yet, river running right on over my head. I wonder if he's still alive? This road seems to wave over low hills forever.

"It's like he's having these blackouts," Denny says. It's not the ceiling of the Sistine Chapel I'm seeing. That's just an emotional reaction to the vaulting, macroscopia, a side effect of the morning-glory injections.

"You seem agitated," I say to them. I suspect I've missed something.

"You collapsed." Scry smiles. Or maybe she looks worried. It's difficult to focus.

I sit up. "Yeah, that happens. Usually the cat licks my face till I wake up—where is she?"

∘ ∘ ∘

The gray women's refuge is a place of rock roses, a break in the pneumatic radiation. No one knows our human names, the silence of paradise. We borrow the women's eye, an eye that can read the alphabet of trees. As a Sybyl I have often sought this opportunity, as a lover neglected it terribly, as a Muscovite short of bread I have fetched stones in hope of soup from it. I have been hiding in all the rabid corners, sucked the rays from those alien faces.

Boar-like, we blow up the Pope's High Road, traverse the Throat with Many Compass Points and burn down Drawing Place House. The besotted Frankish Lord grows surly regarding use of the castle, so we murder him, which delights the Lord's only begotten son, who laughs his baals off. The son feels liberated, and so do we. As he ignites there is general debauchery and population addiction by all. We have a theory that humans are as quotidianly mercurial as fundamental particles, and address each other thus: Quark; Neutron Plus; Bogon from a suxed up Detroit. Howzit, Lepton? Fux m'brainzout, Charm. Beauty is rarely available for interviews, and keeps snake heads in her backpack.

Alice Athena reflectively drives our whirling barques across the sea of the Gobi on temperate westerlies, an animal power in the insubstantial air, sometimes rising to great heights, wings that stomp and snort, buck and gallop, catching a stratospheric tail wind and making it as far as the Mojave.

Hermes Trigonometry yells, "By Jupiter and Danaë!" and a wave of nymphs blush forth with curvy troves.

"Don't look now, but—" gray-eyed Oreades whispers, and all the nymphs fall silent, waiting to hear the words.

"We attack at dawn."

We stop for the night at the home of Eris Harkus, out in Dreamland, near Twentynine Palms.

∘ ∘ ∘

There's a wall and Armamentia and I have to climb it when suddenly it all comes back to me: it's like we're children again, looking for Atlantis and the books that came before it, in the library, a photograph of an alluring island queendom sirening us through the door of the past and into the unexplored fringes of the imagination where the light is always pearly and the goer best step with fissure dread. Kinetic ontology hibernates, and with each foothold up I move closer to the source. The card catalog is at the top of the wall, and the crone librarian is reaching down to pull Armamentia up from the lower depths. The old woman's centaur holds, her flanks rippling, her tail half-erect. The clues are on the yellowed cards not stained and chewed from use of years by common desire—just ask the blue-haired maid *Where's the crazy eight?* and you'll get a boost from below. The gangsters, game players all, pyramid Denny to where he can give me the leg up I need.

Scrambling my eggs, I squirm to the top of the wall. And look out at what's beyond.

Tartary, this green and pleasant land where hell was spawned? These ancient rolling hills like a mother's worn-down molars the cradle of invasions? The ancestors of the inhabitants of those few faraway yurts the progenitors of hordes? Or am I blinding on the transmission from a chain-link antenna surrounding a deserted Colorado high school?

I get off the fence and keep moving. *Keep your perspective.* Things far away don't look so distant, like a rear-view mirror that reflects the future. It's not a schoolyard; it's a hydropower station and we're on the dam. From this angle I can see gangsters straggling up a wall *and* over a fence—maybe I'm not so forgetful after all. Karma oils history, and if we don't succeed we'll be reincarnated in an aquarium.

∘ ∘ ∘

I turn the corner and almost step in a still-stewing hill of cat vomit, cankerous with partially digested gray fur. I know we are on the right trail.

"We're here," Scry says. Denny, Uncle Lucifer and Margarine catch up, Gwenny and the dawn knot climb to the crest and see the cavernous gated entrance of Styx Valley, snatch now the veil from that veiled king. The death-owl doth sing to the night-mares as they go. We see a fire descending in the sky above, a portent of war.

There is a key in the door, which I experience the guilty pleasure of turning, a woman I've never seen before, or don't remember, whispering in the same unintelligible way, all the time, in my ear. The door opens quite softly, and within stands my father, his face white and malignant, and glaring close to mine. He cries in a terrible voice, "Death!" Out go Gwenny's and Scry's candles, and at the same moment, with a scream, I walk into the dark.

∘ ∘ ∘

I can hear all the leaders banging on the drums of our various reasons, Israfel's trumpet blast, this blood lust subservient not even to volcanoes and glaciers, echoing like TVs in the fifth floor of a department store. I scrabble around in the dirt of the cave, trying to find her in the dark. Birds, I have parted you from your cages; now show me her face and declare where she is. Last evening our elephant remembered India again; in a frenzy he was rending the veil of night till dawn. The mirror is ghosting over— when I blow upon it, it protests against me.

"The robots following us are at least twenty years too late, glaucoma in the public eye." Someone in the Open Mike gang knows this, flying a kite with the tail knots tied in code.

"'Tis a nude day," Really Joe says, walking through the Pleiadian arch set in the granite wall. This night we burn down the walls with self-immolating elves, the epileptic affect embroiled in burning a myth, a protest so profound it requires the manifestation of the non-existent. A cunnian sybyl slowly masturbates, her dreaming mind far away.

Grab my flashlight from the door; wreck the car's interior; all this busted-up Oneirica's a witness: the satellites are feeding the museophagic aliens.

∘ ∘ ∘

Denny is hunching down a blacked-out corridor, Scry

right beside him, and it's so dark she holds his shirt tails to keep from losing him.

Invisible rabbits dashing down a tunnel full of lasers and wicked things that tick, *it's later than you think*, we are racing to explode the brain of the octopus, still living, the collaborationist government hiding beneath Styx Valley.

Scry backpacks the little black cube that houses Ginja the virus code, a lapcache, a hundred flavors of operating system, the Baby loRad and trigger. Denny shoulders our food supply, the crone book, and an ancient hemp rope heavier than water. I am lucky to be carrying myself.

"We must remember the passwords as we acquire them," Scry says urgently. *Aquaknowledge.* She slots the virus vector media into her lapcache. She wants Ginja hot and gooey by the time we get to the core. *Strange hellish shit.*

"We just have to get through that revolving door." Denny points dead ahead. The entry to the hollow Earth.

∘ ∘ ∘

Denny is entering from far below, into the lower caverns beneath Styx Valley. Wondering where the generals keep their starship, worrying that he'll have to deliver the virus himself, fearing improvisation. *Aspire deeply.* He signals back to Scry the come-ahead. He pushes through the revolving door, and a quaking alarm like a billion panicked bats shrieks to fill the endless room, thundering like the fall of the tower of Babel, a word so long that only the death of the crier can end it.

∘ ∘ ∘

Denny is trapped behind the debris-stuck door, and the light of the approaching Necks is growing toward us.

"Run!" he yells at Scry, eyes pleading.

Screaming, she slams her fists into the glass of the jammed revolving door that separates them, again and again, but fears there's nothing she can do. The door is like an immobile glacier, unfathomably made of the weakest thing, slow sand icily ticking a knell, an impenetrable alien architecture. As the Necks shuffle nearer, she knows they'll tie her to the mast to witness Denny's death.

Agonized, Scry pauses heartbeat long and lofts the future, sees the huge scope of the invasion, feels Eve's regret. The only way out of the Garden is through the door of betrayal. She remembers Denny kissing every inch of her as many days or nights or noons as he could. She wrestles with the demon Strable for control of the vehicle. Denny can see the reflection of the pool Scry is looking into, *so why can't she break through the glass?*

"Go!"

Scry grabs her pack and runs back up the long tunnel, a woman weeping.

I am crouching shadow still and not remembering where I am.

∘ ∘ ∘

Denny says a prayher to Aquaknowledge:

"O, our bendingray fraction of polarities face-on-face, wear crotchtaped twogather in Her name, good giving tête of mind, the bodely well secretions. O, bending unfractious fellowluster, slip in on slyfox twister-tongue; sheen on shame on, give me straight of melon, nape of good corn, and try'll be happy. Who evermore shallsee nameher, wholehe par religamantarum, a bed we'll share then: you will, I ill, but we be all wells deep, and myth Being ring."

And then he slams his fists once more against the jammed revolving glass door. This time it shatters. Just as the Necks appear around the pillars of stalactites, Denny scrambles through the broken prison door and high-tails it after Scry, but I'm already gone with the wind.

∘ ∘ ∘

I dream I'm swirling my tongue around KOH's Part of Fortune when the earthquake hits. At first I think she's coming, but then I open my eyes. The cat has discovered a sunken empire beneath the horizon and returns to lead the way, licking my face. I wake up in the war-torn Hyatt, but with a lurch see Denny falling. I leap after him.

Scry is running like a wind down a mountain, men must remember. The Open Wound gang foams around her. Margarine relieves Scry of her pack with the Baby IoRad, and the motley crew surges underground.

The psychic explosion takes us all by surprise. A cesium flashcube goes off and there's Yod standing, pointing a camera. For a moment everything is clear as a bell, and then opacity descends from above.

After a few frame-frozen breaths, Scry stumbles back the way she's just come, unpredicting herself as she goes.

∘ ∘ ∘

"Are you KOH?" The dim blue light makes it impossible to see anything but vague outlines. Scry hopes the figure in front of her isn't a robot or hypertrophic Neck.

"Those are my initials. Who—?"

"Friend. Friend to the end. Now let's cast a spell to get out of here, shall we?"

"Antheros?" *Answering love.*

Scry pulls a small cloth bag out of her pocket and hands it to KOH.

"Put your nose in that and take a big snuff."

"Pothos?" *Longing toward the unattainable.*

"We have to extemporalize, and the herbs will help. Please hurry."

Scry pulls out a vial and sprinkles the contents, save a few drops, into KOH's hair. She pulls KOH to her feet, takes the bag and inhales powdered leaves and burnt bones, empties the vial onto her own hair, encircles KOH with her arms.

"I know somebody who loves you." Scry whispers, then sighs, trying to ward off the fear with a show of strength.

KOH smiles, and tilts her head quizzically.

"Himeros?" *To be grasped in the heart of the moment.*

Styx Valley folds inside out, kicks them both in the head by the skins of their teeth.

KOH is tesseracted clear to Hawai'i. She comes to in a meadow in the Pacific-wide shadow of Rose Mountain, the Open Mouth gang in contorted, dislocated heaps all around her. She gets up, shakes the dust off, and starts checking gangsters for broken bones.

"I don't think I'm in Colorado anymore," she whispers to no one, but can't resist looking over her shoulder.

Scry is dashing down a blacked-out tunnel, her Geiger counter a manic metronome of time fleeing before superior forces, the walls tearing at her with memories escaping from the wounded tentacle, her blonde hair ripping from her skull in ravaged knots, her lips tasting a faint trail of psions from Denny's musky soul, terror pumping her legs through the pitch as the corrupt valley surrounding her begins to collapse like a bad seed's destiny.

○ ○ ○

Forwarding motion, technotsunami waving straight at me, result of a culturequake. The volcanic kundalini spine keeps rearing up from the grave, sitting bolt in the middle of things, more fool me grinning rictus sardonicus. Splurgelusting, forwarding motion, like a planetary orbit or duckling imprinting. Nine lives are not enough, come again and again, all innocence and battered knowledge bedded together and sprouting contradictions from the mycelium. A thousand labels fly; not one is the name, even to the individual. Nicht, nought, noir, Gordian knot is where we are.

I can't say it in plainer words. Everything I see is tied together in a fibrous matrix of light. Some can tell stories; others of us are stuck weaving enthymemes and peeling onions, shedding tears for what must be done but wasn't.

No label can hold what it contains: there is always for-warding motion. *Are you really there?* I seem to be always asking. *Are you thinking of me?* To essay is to assay, to dis-cover the contents and make-up of something, to explore that which no label can hold. Seven Chinese boys swal-low the ocean. Pop eats itself. Tourism is imperialism. Everything all the time, forwarding motion.

Storytelling, any kind of narrative, the time it takes a falling body to light, is a ritual of cannibalism, contact—consensus- or coercion-making—creating a clipping path for consciousness. The filter of the mind against the venom of the aliens. Chaos is not entropy; wandering aimlessly is an arrival. The serpent rises, from the bowels to the brain, appending through fingers and tongues. *Denny, can you hear me?* Meaning rests in the ground, and we dig it up in the physical world, with pick axes or camel-hair brushes, in spieling contemplation or edge-jumping exaltation. The ground is the grunt of understanding. The ground is the third eye.

Some say that someday the Lunarians or Pleiadians or Elvis will come back and save us, unite us into a bland soup of new-age DNA, happy-blind as grubs glutting in a log. I don't like stories from which I cannot recover my difference, people that talk that line are trying to shut me up. Difference is pepper, unpredictable sneezes. It's the cultural oil that lubes us up for the fucking we're going to take. I rather like the sensation. It has a certain forward-ing motion.

◦ ◦ ◦

"The passwords!" Scry is screaming at us from across the chasm. *"Say the passwords!"*

Denny and I turn simultaneously, where gather two or more, at last make eye contact and yell at each other, "Barbar, tartar, borbor!" The bonds that bind him to my future release. He clutches Scry calling him back to her as a door slams closed between us. *But is he free?* Did I just break up with Scry?

All is dark. I can feel the sux undoing my bonds. First my hair, then my skin, my molecules are rising, splitting up in order to cover more ground, rushing upwards into a bright-pink sound voluptuous as a Siren.

It is the Mothership.

Sin á Gog

I DREAM OF SHIVERING AWAKE AND SEEING her face smiling down at me, of KOH somehow finding me. I awake with the rocks, heaving in the hold. I can hear the ship creaking as it presses through the nine billion names, I am a minnow tossed. Am I strapped to an interspace console in a starship, mooned by aliens?

Madonna Curie comes in with tea. So this is how they do it. I gaze intently at what the busty pseudodame is cooking over a plasma jet in her bent-handled tablespoon. Arrayed before 'dame are a glass of spring water (she pinches in a blink of bleach), a cotton ball, and a baker's dozen microfine insulin syringes. In case she doesn't get it right the first time?

I can't see the sides of the room—where am I? Janis Joplin sidles up to me from out of the woolly depths of the Mothership.

"Lord, won't you buy me a new personality," she warbles like a loon fishing in her favorite lake.

"J- J- J-Loop?" I stutter, nauseous from the dystemporalia, terrified of what might happen next. Curie, fortunately, is intent on her scientific work.

Janis locks her eyes with mine.

"Barbar, tartar, borbor," she whispers.

"I'm so happy to hear you say that." I want to give her a come-to-Vegas kiss on the lips, but I'm tied to the mast. "Aquaknowledge has answered my prayher. Can you get me out of here?"

"Yes. But not until the aliens desire the sux again. That's when they drop their shields."

"How often?"

"Every three days or so. You've already been here a day. Do you remember any of it?"

I've heard that line before. I shrug, unable to verbally commit.

"They're mind-wiping you, extracting your memories to use as paradigm generators for the false consciousness they broadcast to the general population. Physiologically you will be unharmed, but psychologically..."

I gulp. Maybe they'll figure out how boring I am, the way Armamentia did. "Is there anyone else alive up here?"

Janis nods. "The astronomer, Nairbula. They're not having much luck with him. His root memories are truncated."

"He's a bifurcated personality," I say. "One of mine. I have to find my old lover. We have a telepathic link strong enough to block the aliens' psi-band emissions if we can reunite for long enough to get it going. So I split up in order to cover more ground. But the aliens got her, too."

"No, I know who you mean. She's safe now on Hawai'i. Scry pulled her out of Styx Valley right before the Omnimutational Gang reached the core with the Baby loRad."

"I remember an explosion. I thought I was..." Irish eyes are smiling. *A pennyroyal for your thoughts.* I hear KOH calling me to her, *I want you so much.*

"It was a strange moment for all of us. I have to go. Don't give up."

She disappears in a mist of translucent scarves.

Madonna Curie approaches with the needle.

∘ ∘ ∘

"Changeling, mutant, chimera!" I can hear children

yelling, taunting, breaking open my viscera with sonic spikes spitting off their tongues. Madonna Curie tweaks a setting with a discolored fingertip and the spikes rape into me, jagged edges ripping, sawing through everything unseen. And then it stops.

"What year is this?" Curie demands. She has the texture of Einstein's hair tile-filling the very air, oozing along on the teakwood floor.

"It's a green year. It has no name," I reply, the mother of fact.

Amanuensis Einstein materializes on the poop deck, and is gazing down at me. I can't read his face. He may be transreal, cellular automata, an artist's impression.

"Wrong. This is your human Year of Living Dangerously." She clicks her heels together three times. Nothing happens. "Why did you throw the potassium in the swimming pool?" *You're going to feel a little pinch.*

There is a double-fist lump of fear in my throat. I cannot speak; I cannot face this. What I want to know is, does this mean my memories are mine? *Or not?* It's not what I did, but what I said. "Tony's strung out. He's crazy. You're better off without him." The words shoot through my brain like a fast-acting drug. That's the point, I guess: don't be afraid to love or you'll get locked down in a mental starship prison. *Just a tiny pinprick.*

∘ ∘ ∘

Radon, produced by disintegration of radium, discovered by the Furies, fogs at the feet of their prey. Somewhere far off softly plays an inexorable duet, a pulsing rove of hyphenated body rhythms. The omniscient lights surge, cycling darkness in counterpoint with illumination. Am I cascading?

Missionary numchucks whirl past my ears. I dive in a low but high-energy parabola around some core algorithms in the Mothership's cachenet. The numchucks buzz overhead, hurled in orbit-disintegrating frustration, and gut through the working files of a superstore in Floating Manhattan, wrecking everything, creating long lines at checkout counters. I could almost get out of here on my own, except who threw that?

Demon if they will, possession if I can, I turn to Mnemosyne with the empty squad cars ever remaining at throat-hold by the cuckolding syntax, the clutches of a simpleton's letter-beat box, nine-tenths of the Law. It was I who held the peach of KOH; ever more she'll be to do what thou wilt. A zonecall with rhythmic drumming, a biosemiotic few bytes of chemistry thirsting through the brain, entraining on Curie's strobing beacon...

The ravings which my enemy utters I hear within my heart; the secret thoughts he harbors against me I also perceive. His dog bit my foot. He showed me much injustice. I do not bite him like a dog; I bite my own tongue. Since I have penetrated into the secrets of individuals like men of the Goddess, why should I take glory in having penetrated his secret? I reproach myself that through my doubtings it so happened I drew a scorpion towards my own foot.

Like Adam, whom Necks see nothing of except his fire, I am invisible to these insignificant Necks. Convey to my friends that I am afflicted in mind; when the snake bit my thigh I started away from the black rope. The blessed ones closed their lips and eyes. By a way unknown to any man, I ran into their thoughts; since there is a secret way from heart to heart, I gathered gold and silver from the treasuries of hearts.

Take it as if I had not ever spoken these words; if I had been in your mind, by Goddess, I would not have stolen.

Curie orders me to discuss sense, but I can only come up with strands. *I'm an image, Ma'am, an onion of interpretation.* I can hear the Mothership whirling in dead languages, some mumbled words learned when wandering Persian scholars traded dictionaries with Hibernian monks. I'm scared shitless, afraid that everything I know is wrong.

"It is always illuminating to have a new history with which to examine one's past." The aliens are amalgamating me, trying to make me steal *and* pure. "What's wrong— cat got your tongue?"

"No." I gulp air. "I'll tell you, just let me catch my breast I mean breath I mean brisées—"

∘ ∘ ∘

Cattle rustling, key stealing, the lyre's recompense, ball and chain, *what was it?* We were hitchhiking, I remember how this goes, Lydia and me stuck in Bakersfield when Hermes picked us up, drove us all the way to Merced. Uncle John's bandits, we smoked and sussed and scryed the pools of each other's steel-glinted eyes, the heavy-metal addiction that had us on the road in the first place, heading northwest to get fixed. Our poverty and desperation came clear to Hermes as Lydia slept in the back seat. He hatched a raven's trickster plot of revenge, grand theft, to victimize his brother's cattle ranch from which he'd just been laid off. Selling the beasts at auction'd bring a nest egg to take to Cern Francisco, get even higher. So went the roar. We struck before dawn.

Through a pitch-black irrigation ditch in acres of mud, we slogged to the outer limits of the pens, lifted latches and from under the mother's pillow stole two key calves.

"Put your fingers in its mouth, like this. The calf'll think it's a teat and follow you anywhere," Hermes said, psychopomp and pay the circumstances.

Holding the power of sux by stealth we led the calves away when suddenly all the lines changed at once.

Slapped back onto our beshitting asses, the lights came on hard and fast, a video camera aimed at our faces.

Hermes' brother Apollonaire charged straight at Lydia, a gun in his other hand pointed at my chest.

"I'm going to fuck you," he snarled at Lydia, and then turned to me and Hermes, "and kill both of you. Now, who wants to go first?"

Lydia and I stood treestump still, but instead of answering, Hermes started to dance like he'd just invented music, a frenzy that soon began to ooze out of his mouth and drip down onto his already brackish T-shirt. Apollonaire snatched up his brother's shirt front, gnashing, "You epifuckenleptic son of a nymph!" and started slapping Hermes' face.

Pulling and dragging each other, Lydia and I ran ungracefully back to the road. I lost a shoe to the mud, but we stole Hermes' car.

That was the springtime of our coin drop, a luck that sucked and tugged us through the quotidia of night and day, dream and duration. It would be difficult to convict on a felony if the jury doesn't perceive a crime as having been committed. *Jesus Crustacean, gitcher cripe-mongering aquarium cameras out of my thermador.* Nairbula... I wonder if Joanne Mansfield still sleeps with her arms up. *The world is everything that is the case.* The demon Strable.

o o o

Amanuensis Einstein approaches the command cache console and nods at it, arms and legs akimbo. He is invincible—I remember Dr. Sax telling me this as part of my therapy, or maybe it was in one of her books—like Superman and Jesus rolled into one. He reminds me of Aristotle, for some reason.

Einstein pulls out his cock and begins urinating on the hypercurious cachement. Or maybe Diogenes, kynics are for kids, silly rarebyte. The overdose of salty metals leaks in on ham gravity. The control units simper and gasp, knees knocking, guts oozing gooily through kinetic nostrils, one shuddering shiver like the final smack pay back, and then the alien cachement ceases functioning.

I feel a weight lift suddenly from my shoulders; my birds take flight. Einstein gathers me in his arms, lifts me, strokes my cheek.

"Come, my anomalous little Earthling. This is no place for you."

I am falling vast through the Mothership, weaker than water, K—no, I ride in Einstein's arms. Such hallucinations are a side effect of all the drugs I've taken. Been forced to take. After effect. I see Scry sitting in a Hummer emblazoned with the Karma Sumatra logo. But there is no Karma Sumatra logo, is there?

"Any messages?" I ask, then—

∘ ∘ ∘

—I may have drifted. The last thing I remember is— Am I chained to the wall of a dungeon? Where's Scry? KO—

∘ ∘ ∘

What is her name? I pray for predictions, begin to get the picture of narrative eruptions along our fault lines that join us together two by two or more in Her name gathered. Scry can barely suss me; she tries to explain to Denny just what it is I'm trying to say. Between the ancient creation of the world and its possible end today, the discussion about matter begins with classical antiquity, whose radiant legacy is an inextricable part of our minds. Plato celebrates it. Aristotle, the Stoics, and Plotinus join in. The light is seen to descend into their heads in rings of golden fire. The church father Augustine makes this talk the foundation of his systemic explanation of the creation from nothingness, an explanation that has become doctrine among orthodox aliens, currently showing at the Blue Purie.

Einstein presses the big green button. I begin to make

copies of myself.

Libra maniacs Corsican in their precise and serious instruments. Astrum Aster! *Here we come!* Voodoo haiku, culting through all the blathering heat waves, best friends and lovers left in the dusty mud, thumbs saluting the sky.

Gravity—it's more than just a fragrance. Did this really happen? Who can truly see back through the foggy myths, even if it all happened only yesterday, with the aliens swimming in the TVs that hurricane my eyes into the whirling vat of the Mothership? I am dyed blue in the wool, and sewn into a quilt. Dying is an acid bath for the mercurial soul; death is a web, ions after eons. Nairbula adjusts the Newtonian focus of the telescope, reflective in chains. In the past twenty-three years he's lost thirty-three friends to the transgenic terrorist. From outer space. *A litany, those names*, old Nairbula thinks. They may not be spoken, but how they echo, like some Irish or Sufic tune.

Interpsychic cross fade, I can't quite hear Nairbula. I wish I could connect with Denny or Scry. I have a feeling Einstein and Curie are just calibrating their equipment, that this is just a sound check.

"That's right, open the window," Amanuensis Einstein says. "You want to know the truth? The truth is you can live forever. Come inside with me and I'll show you. We're making martyr sauce. If that's what you call something that rises from the dead and lives underground. Eternal life for those who believe in us, hell fire for those who don't. And the apocalypse is coming on Earth, any day now."

An ineffable light shines round Einstein and Curie, and the dead body of Tony Cross springs upright. Taking in his hand the head of a corpse, Tony proceeds to the exposition of the kinds of torture used by the aliens. These torments, including the shooting of humans with telepathic arrows, is attested by the biographies of many martyrs, particularly of the two hundred and sixty million, whose names are unknown to us, but who are recorded by Victor in his *Tartar Persecution*. Irenis, Christina, Sebastian, Christopher and Faustus all died in this fashion, of which the last record is given in the Greek *Menology* of August 15 of the Year of Whitewater.

"The Blessed Martyr, Saint Faustus, under the Producer Spellbottom, by reason of his confession, was arrested. Freely professing himself as one who had deliberately yanked his own implant, he was fixed to a cross and wounded with arrows. On another occasion the Springtide rites were being celebrated, and the people having met in a place called the Telesterion to honor Spring Day, shut and locked the temple upon themselves. The aliens discovered this. Immediately one of their Necks, Anonymous by name, collecting together a band of armed pseudanthropes, started to attack the party of innocent worshippers. The Necks rushed in with drawn swords, and some of them, climbing up to the roofs, shot showers of arrows through the granite niches of the temple. Just then, as it befell, Aquaknowledge's people were singing, and a reader was standing in the pulpit intoning the hallelujah vesicle. At that moment an arrow caught him in the throat, and the book fell from his hand, as he, too, fell down dead."

When the speech is done, the martyr goes down to the appointed place, and blinding his eyes with a branding iron given him two days before, and kneeling down as though in prayer, ends his martyrdom and his orisons at one and the same time by kneeling down and stretching out his neck.

Internalized spiritual war carried on since then, the history of the cranial jail house where the aliens first came and nabbed the verb, poor mad prince, subjected to such shocking treatment. Do I see interrogators gathering on the purple ridge?

There is an out-building with a crescent mooning on the poop deck, in front of which looms the revolted

Alaric—and suxwise Kalium is the Latin cognac, mescalinerally speaking, that sumerized his flesh back onto his bones—his atmanic cymbals crushing my hears, I had come to ship and only parted, in front of me standing, metal teeth and all, Alaric the Astralgoth, a Phish Christ in a specimen bowl dangling from his neck. I try to run but am tied to the mast when a siren goes off—

Strable is the heir to Babylon, the Eater of the Apple, the Translator. This is what the demon means, as grapheme and trope: to consume greedily, the *nevertheless* sign, the unthinkable thus real ratcheting of fear, gravel for grovel. The one who makes me say, *Of course you're right*, and beg for more, legs weak as water on a road less travelled, logos bifurcated, pneuma from psyche. Teleos the interloper, optically self-aware cachement, what multiply addictive errors have arisen in the channelings of our own self-diagnoses. Tell the Inquisitor of the Demonstration that the Gaian brain transcends the sum of any nomenclature. Strable is not noise. Strable is evidence of breathing together, and Alaric is heaving joyously greedy breaths.

Strable is the monster's breath on my neck, my face on fire with the smell of burning villages. *This is serious.* Remember the new forget the old. Denny can't see me, Scry is a faraway patch of granite fog, psions sparking. Disavow any knowledge, shred me like a clear-cut, and we'll do lunch. Just get me out of here before the deep dish bakes me.

○ ○ ○

Charles Mingus rode a dream-mare shortly after Joni impregnated him. He got up out of bed and composed a reedy and sinuous sonata for cello and bagpipes, the injection of which kicks back at the TV, this black boomerang ricocheting off my chest. The alien hand flashes *Don't Walk*, and means it.

"Just lie still. Tell us what we want to know."

The Astralgoths sacked Times Roman. There were a lot of anti-mnemon particles floating around. I may have accidentally inhaled some when the terrorists exploded the building—heads will roll—vaporizing a pea of convulsium-137. Nobody knew what temperature it was. All I can say at this time is that I have nothing further to add.

"We have ways—"

I can see their telescoping ions peering at me through the murky water. I want to fuck and bifurcate, but so far away from here. I seem to be a prisoner. I remember something—Alaric is standing before me.

"You recognize my face." He still bears the cheeky scar where a graphic designer, fighting for her sex life, slashed him with a pair of scissors from a drawing program.

"Agnosia only goes so far, I'm afraid."

"I'm here to torture you, you know."

"Then I'm sure you'll accomplish your task quite handily. Wake me when it's over."

Alaric begins to chant. It's like a Chinese water drill—his heart just isn't in the right place, and he pronounces the words all wrong, tortures them. Perhaps that's the point, fingernails on a blackboard screeching, slapping me every time I drift off to sleep. *Hey, buddy, there's a message for yuh.* Alaric stands with arms akimbo.

"I'm going to suck your soul out through your asshole."

A brand is heating in a nearby brazier. Alaric pulls it out of the yellow-hot coals. The iron A is so super-heated it blinds white, and an orange fire descends from above.

∘ ∘ ∘

I am gasping for emancipation. The aliens never sought our approval, and we never asked what they were doing. *A broad cast of thousands.* They descend with a light as bright as magnesium burning. It radiates into our heads like blue X-rays, but they swear this is all just a graphical metaphor. A user interspace. No need to get excited, they say, their lies so banal, like butter—"ways of making you talk."

The ratchet of drugs, stolen alchemical formulæ, abuses, pacts beyond all skirmish of reason—all into the pool. Cat, Bear, Owl: we gave them mall we bought, forest floaters, smoking bowlers, scrotum-shrinking squint and run. The big news is tribal semiotics have been wiped out with a quiver full of barbs and sharpened tongues. The spiritual-analogy cachepit is now a midden.

The conditions of these rising and fading tones are irretrievably singular, like the circumstances from which a dream might arise. I imagine that even someone standing nearby would experience these torturous demons as though pressed, an exile, against a pane of glass as life passes in reflected images, filling the entire pane, which cannot be entered, like the space in a mirror.

During pounding ketamine-induced hallucinations I dream of swords. I remember a long journey across the Amanita shamanlands, mares running, manes of fire. *Don't let them do this to you.* I seem determined to cross-examine the aliens responsible, but first I must remember where they put me. *The Mothership sux—say it three times.* From a garroted window I can see the purple hills rumpling under the tender mercies of the furnace being wheeled across the tablelands.

Stay true to your images. But while supplies last Alaric intromissively cranks the knob to VHF.

○ ○ ○

"Do I cast a shadow—or does a shadow cast me?"

Judy Garland flips her feather boa at the Ontological Missionairies crowded in the cabin of a yacht, pacificlly drifting. It's a loopy thing Judy occasionally does. When Alaric sticks a fork in my fillings, I start to pick up the gangsters' simulcast. Although it seems only one of them,

Phrixus Andronicus, has ever sailed before. A drifter, a tiny pink feather, tickles Margarine Not Butter's nose. Ms. Garland has photos, to everyone's delighted amazement, of the largest collection of hotel towels in the known universe, and a floor-to-ceiling bookcase crammed tightly with Gideon Bibles. I begin to crow in excitement. Alaric looks puzzled. Flying is sympathetic magic. Judy drives a dymaxion car and packs her meager treasure on a skeptical goat.

"The great revenge—so don't look now," Judy's hips swing in emphasis, "will be Harmonia's, the mediatrix whose bats dart through tangles of our hair, the taste of salt metal as we are forced to consume the excavated remains of Sodom and Gomorrah, and spell our names wrong on government benefits forms for the rest of our lives." The pornographic splines are splitting. The entire invasion is recorded live and the sensation of over-night ratings continues to soar.

None of this is really happening. The thought occurs. I can't seem to close my mouth. I don't remember a thing— or, rather, I remember something else entirely.

I cannot ask questions for fear of being shot, not Shakti, shocked? I feel driven to accept the challenge of living in the world, multivalently compelled to accept near-deaths and life-threatening initiations into trickster fraternities of central Lemurian origin, these things that plague a human life, like weeping for Will long before he ever drowned. Such intuitive knowledge must be acquired quickly in order to survive. There is a crucial death-defying scene with an owl or bear or cat. I must not question Aquabeknowledgment—am I fighting back?

Give me all you've got; the gene paths go ever on. The fat hill's oval orbit yields a lone nut accusing the Astralgoth of unlawfully breaking into a temporal loop and attempting to lock out the fingers of consensual ecstasy. Press the button, baby. Put your foot on it, because this is a greenly lit path to a rosy mound of anarchy, which I, in the burnings of my desire, seek more than anything. I'd like to take back responsibility for my life, to order my heart according to the musings of my own neurotic mythology, instead of having my memories siphoned up an aquarium for alien convergence.

∘ ∘ ∘

Jesus on a binge, how many degrees of initiation can a person go through before being contacted by the Invisible? An accordian somewhere far off wheezes. Fios Eolas Fochmark Khan, knowledge is power. Uncle Lucifer said that, in one of his conspiracy stories. But then the coin toss turns up tales. Three times three to the third degree. What day it is, in media res, has already criminaled the strip-search assault assembly. Lock jaw; insert shunt.

Prisoners are not allowed to comment. Even though defense lawyers are present, the circumstances dissolve the case into sulfur, the prosecutors into civil alchemists. They each piss in a ground-down remedy of the court with bizarre shreds of irreplaceable Moslem texts thrown in at random but demonic time intervals.

Alaric won't let go. Advertising answers all. If you see the Buddha on the road, nail him to a billboard. Studies show. If Yod won't stop pointing at you, then I say *this is the sign you've been looking for*. The saucers would land by Giant Rock. The aliens would come out and exchange small gifts with George van Tassel, out in the desert, there at night. They never gave him any secret plans for a time machine; he made that part up later. The aliens prove to be superb, if devious, cognitive cartographers.

"This is argon. It will not harm you, though it will change your mind. Do not resist the injection." If Rome perishes—one tiny prick and its over—where is safe?

∘ ∘ ∘

Shriek when the pain hits during interrogation. Reach into the Dark Ages to find a sound that is liquid horror, a sound on the brink where man stops and the beast with steel tongues leers and corrals. Scream when your life is threatened. Form a noise so true that your tormentor recognizes it as a voice that lives in his own throat. The true sound tells him that he cuts his flesh when he cuts yours, that he cannot thrive after he tortures you. Scream that he destroys all kindness in you and blackens every vision you could have shown him.

Alaric switches the channel to UHF.

The Astralgoth shatteringly enters through vicious breaking glass, slapping me instantly with his baseball bat. Seeing searing silver, now white, now black, I'm back through the roof of my brain and see Alaric stabbing Armamentia's harmless kitten with his barb-headed eel. She's helpless, screaming, choking beneath the bat he straddles her with. He sees me starting to move and his bat strikes two but I can't die. I'm gasping at the chasm that separates me from my wife. She's weeping, bleeding beneath his slow, brutal pelvis-slamming thrusts. I start to vomit and lift my head. Alaric sees and turns, rips his slathering eel from Armamentia's vagina. Jacking and ratcheting, he points the roaring beast at me and explodes cum in my mouth, a sulfurous geyser scalding my face and eyes, flooding broken teeth and blood down my throat.

As I cascade into unconsciousness I remember I don't recognize this body, a TV staring at me, sated.

∘ ∘ ∘

And a little light goes on?

Don't talk down to me. Don't be polite to me. Don't try to make me feel nice. Don't relax. I'll cut the smile off your face. You think I don't know what's going on. You think I'm afraid to react. The joke's on you. I'm biding my time, looking for the spot. You think no one can reach

you, no one can have what you have. I've been planning
while you've been playing. I've been saving while you've
been spending. The game is almost over so it's time you
Aquaknowledged me. Do you want to fall not ever knowing who took you?

○ ○ ○

Scry must have the Open Mind gang doing a mass telepathy session, beckoned by Aquaknowledge, and ever-
drumming the names of the drowned, the disenchanted,
the diseased, the disowned and disavowed, the lost ones
wandering dissolute in Night Town, the dead, the dismembered, the disoriented, the dateless, the dim-witted ones,
all those too dirty or dangerous to be invited, perhaps especially the deaf, but certainly playing to invoke the displaced memories of wandering aimlessly, playing to remember the forgotten.

They want to pull me down from here, but the alien sux
is truculent, chronic as a bad-habit attitude. Their sweet
tune, reminiscent of a time not so long ago but now forgotten, is drowning in a sea of infamous apathy leaking from
the apartment above. The warehouse in back?

Socrates, an atom in the heel of a giant's boot, asked
Tony Cross, "What proof have you that we are not asleep?
Could this interrogation be the shivers of a dreamer rather
than, as we so blithely assume, two talking in the waking
condition?" Thousands of REM cycles later the question is
still being asked. Tweedledum comments to Alice that the
Red King is dreaming about her and were the King to leave
the building, Alice would be "No where" because she is
only a sort of thing in his dream. When Alice complains
that Tweedledum and Tweedledee's loud talking might
wake the King, Tweedledum counters, "Well, it's no use
your talking about waking him when you are only one of
the things in his dream. You know very well you're not
real." *Nothing is not real*, but my tongue is tied in

interpsychic knots.

Research indicates an osmotic high until three, with gathering weaves of depression to follow through May. We'll raise our umbrellas like mushrooms in the reign of frogs, and long wave the polyversal fag. *Existamatur*, or so we want them to think we think. Einstein can't turn the damned thing off; the very air is starting to smell like an ill-kept aquarium—phone home. I sense the Operation Media gang are searching their hearts for me; they're omming in.

The puzzlement of it all, Scry caresses a notebook full of equations penned with invisible lemon-juice ink only now browning, revealing the edges of the information as she holds the paper over a candle flame. *Here is the telepathic feedback*. Ginja, a name on my tongue. The noise of consciousness makes Heisenberg's uncertainty look like the very principle of logical positivism. *Broadcast on many frequencies to be sure it gets heard*. Or I could be hallucinating.

Or is all this change just a reminder that we are lemurs clinging to the leafing twigs in the jungle genes of initial conditions? No left turn—menstruation, beard, tics, rash, disease, death, fungus, all just behind our ears—nothing a good radiation treatment couldn't erode, or so you'd think, given the ferocity of their anamneses.

∘ ∘ ∘

Shit my can, O, my monkey tekma niacon, digressive polymerization is grabben at my heaving heaven hiven neck of the leg lurching, quit claim versus patrimony, account of narcolepsy, Gerschwind's Syndrome, I need a good enthypoetic epistleotomy. Nylons stretch, is this a lounge? Are these pimps or waitresses? Scientists? Maybe I should've listened to Dr. Sax.

Shut up, or I'll explode your head.

You *are the sux, Alaric.*

Cusp for sale, Scorpio rising. *I can't hear you.* Not too many sun spots, moon negotiable. *Whistle to my cat.* Let it be known throughout the land that this journey has been a fool's errand. I am living in the wrong time again.

Gravity, nuclear, strong, weak— Consciousness is the missing premise. Eros is the other fundamental force. In our search we helix toward what we lack. Embodied, the demonstrable, stuff wants to make more stuff. Enthymemic aposiopesis. The page from *The Thousand and One Voices* appears to have been written in the Vattanian urphabet. The scribe has perfectly copied the original manic script, the turbulent letters and the burns in the paper together.

The sky is bare as the desert. Here are honking crowds gathering ectogangster, zending plasma trance, with necktophiliacs impersonating humans interspersed throughout the crowd and blotting into things, every fucken where the felonious virulence infects jurisprudence. Talk about wear a condom, hire a lawyer, buy a gun, split town. A few geese overhead. Reef transceives e-mail from a wingnut computer scientist who thinks she's discovered a blocking agent, a way to get over the hump and start having human babies again. As a strategy, plasticity is desirable; the danger is of becoming so malleable we assume the shape of our container. *To block what?* Reef types back. *Are you talking about spies playing football?* Scry opens *The Thousand and One Voices* and asks, *Have you seen Silas?*

The third hand is the hand that slaps him awake: it is the clapping hand. *We'll bring the balloon around immediately.*

∘ ∘ ∘

"Go with Peter Gelmanov. He'll take you back to Earth."

An old woman speaks to me—her eyes are Berber gray—tells me all these things. She has a book with her, in a bag in her shopping cart. Which has a warp engine and working headlights that she can blink on and off when she wants to signify. Break the back of breathing clubs conformed of old white men with neatly braided encrustations of glee, greed, and deep breeding. *Is more like it.*

Suddenly I recognize her; she's Jeanne d'Arc, from somewhere in the J-Loop. She's glaring at someone behind me. I scry something of Alaric reflecting in the pools of her eyes. With all my might I snap my wrists out and back, the razor of Alaric's intentions judoing through my bonds, and fleeing I see the grand balloon floating alongside the Mothership. Joan d'Arc drags me forward while the luminous Russian novelist Gelmanov bellows and poetically beckons us to catch the rope ladder dangling from the gondola.

The cat leaps in after me, straight into my arms. She's grinning, but afraid of heights, leaf quivering.

Professor Gelmanov is firing the balloon with radiant plasma. The Optimum Might gang heave sandbags ahoy the sides, some clearly aimed at Curie and Einstein, now copulating, fruitlessly trying to create their own link. Alaric lies in a puddle; it's possible I punctured him with the tines of my forked tongue.

"With the ogres down, why hurry, Dr. Gelmanov?" I ask. "Can you sail this thing over to the main mast? I want to see who's tied up there." *Swing lo—*

"Wait a second. Has anybody seen my baby?" *—sweet baby at?*

Reef is onboard, too?

Do I recognize your voice?

"He has a point," says the professor, piloting his pressurized pile of silk and reeds bulbously down the girth of the Mothership, mainsail breasting just ahead. "Reef commissioned this odyssey."

"With Scry's help. And some intelligent software named Ginja. I'm trying to find Silas Proton. He got pulled up the sux." Reef doesn't seem to recognize my face.

Maybe I don't have one. I'm feeling strangely hyper-distributed, *infectious vectoring*.

No aliens are rushing across the deck, but Nairbula is lashed to the mast. Margarine diskinetics the old soul's bonds, and he nimbly snags the ladder, clambering aboard as the balloon rises up and away from the Mothership. He pats his caftan as if trying to remember where he put something.

"You're a brilliant man to have tried, Reef." I can *feel* Silas, but don't want to say anything to Reef. The sense of Silas is in the mix of the alien soup, blanched and peeled, memory enhanced and discorporated.

Reef says nothing, leaning against the gondola bulkhead like somebody's sawed off two of the legs of his tripod. Phrixus touches his cheek, tender.

Feather and yoni, my hands on your body are a hula song.

Suddenly, I remember I have to be somewhere.

"Can you get this balloon to Hawai'i?" I ask Gelmanov.

"We can float this baby to Mars, if you're not in a hurry."

"I want to go to Mauna Loa."

"That would be an active volcano in the Pacific."

"Right."

"Mondo choppy air. But okay." Gelmanov looks at me side long, piercing. "Something's riding you like a horse."

Loa unto thee, you who cop me from behind, suck this sign!

"You got it. Just call me Mare Nontranquilium. You can say that again, yes sir, and I'm late for a very important date."

Gelmanov laughs as if beset by a medical condition, the plasma torch blazing above his head. He shoves his curly hair away from the back of his neck, turns grinning, "I shunt never be implanted." His neck's weathered and wrinkled, but nary a prick.

"It's a good idea," Nairbula says casually. "I do believe I lost aboard the Mothership a Baby loRad I was smuggling. I'm sure I did. I think. And I set it to go off a few minutes from now. Or days that might have been."

"Let's luau!" Gelmanov cries. "The Hawai'i Express. We'll be descending through naughty bits of the Pacific atmosphere, full of falling command posts. But right by the observatory is that Rose Mountain you gangsters have been chattering about. Must admit, I'm a little curious myself."

Nairbula smiles, polishing his lenses. The gangsters exchange high-fives.

Donning a black eye patch, Gelmanov proves to be the source of the story that pirates are kind to children, and that a faithful companion is empire enough, that, and the sea ether air.

Apocalypse Tao

TAKE HER DOWN TO BARE FEET per second squared and to Tartary with the pressure. Every time I swallow my body does a subsave, auricular write function; ear-popping lungs have keepsakes. Bopping through the toxic and radioactive molecules, aglistening we do Earthward fall. Pico-curious, we harbinger the nuggets of atomic fame; tiny curies of radiation fatten us up. Lamb time, throat space, we convulse the bolus uphill, just to watch it roll back down the gullet of gravity. Science wants to know even that which has been rinsed away with soap. I will now return to my normal size.

The weight on my eyes—I may explode into little pieces. Give me that slathering rag and an in-flight magazine, try'll be happy. The hull of the gondola is lined with aloe, but I don't trust the looping scaldrons of molten atmosphere that go searing past. The ride's like slamming something on fire, noxious, a metallic taste in my mouth, not to mention a head ringing like my skull is cast from bronze. The silk balloon has a mile-long drag line howling above us, finally slowing the whole gangster bang down. On-site experts estimate a crew of eighty, drifting into the silk-stocking shot below.

They're lovely, lounging, wearing lingerie, proterra noun

mounds, nipples peeping through cloud-weaved fabric, hiding their necrogenital forces beneath mod lava skirts, volcanic omphallos and vulva. Land ho.

"Rose Mountain's on the big island," I say to Dr. Gelmanov, perhaps needlessly.

"It's not in the Mall of America," he replies.

"Between Mauna Loa and Hualalai."

"Right tow."

"Pu'u Keanui," I say the Hawai'ian name for Rose Mountain.

"Gotta have it."

"The missionaries only gave them eight letters," I apologize. I may be forgetting how compressed time is here. Was I the missionary? Or did I tender the map that marked the missionary's position?

Our descent, at first like a fire from above, is now a petal lilting downwards, gliding in to fill the lei. We tumble out of the gondola onto the sharp black sand, and Margarine sets up the mike.

○ ○ ○

I am given a peanut butter and jealousy sandwich for breakfast. It's an emotional iceberg in the path of my thin-plate sidings, a scribbled nebulation of all I wish or fear. I chew fantasies of women I'll never meet, and so every woman stirs my receptors; I must search every face for the one I haven't met or for the one I long ago wronged and left. Or could I travel back in time, kick my own ass, and teach myself to do the right thing? *Where is Scry?* That was KOH's voice. This time I'm sure. Raw, yet refined, like turbinado sugar, my Venus is in hot water. I shed my shell.

How do we meet again? Reporters have nothing better to do; they chop off fingers to chum the telequarium waters. The Open Mike gang is sweeping the area, yanking implants as they go. Out they pop like zits, leaving an oozing bead of oil, just a little something to soothe the friction. Suddenly, all the TVs in Hilo die silent, quickly collapsing into dust and then disappearing with an implosive sux. This is genuine progress.

It is on a busy street where we meet again, islands of surprise in the streaming crowd. "Cinnamon and tiger oil!" KOH cries, and I can see the alien accretions cascading from her mind; she remembers a scent that lifted her spirits long ago, the synesthesic memory tugging the continent of her existence.

I pause at the corner, habitually looking to the alien for the signal to walk or stop, and there she is, staring at me like an owl.

"Kat—!" I cry, but my tongue freezes, I can't bear to say her name, not yet, not here. Instead, I run to close the distance between us.

I take her in my arms and kiss her lips, glimpse the roaring world in silence. She takes me back, stretching up to meet me like a cat, her face the hunger that whets our lengthening feast.

KOH is beautiful, as compelling as gravity. She wears her clothes like a flock of birds, a frizzy-haired, starry-eyed woman riding me on her Halley-Davidson motorcomet, a swift fish in the slipstream of missing time, like mushrooms we psi lost fringes, Sybylday shine run, her just-so gaze of brown, sweet tears answer like this is true, her kiss is to take my soul the wind to keep, ache for indigo as sensitive as a tongue, my missing secret ingredient, my just-add-water, my mother's recipe for the cure, my nubile beginning.

◦ ◦ ◦

A day contained between two other days, no night without stars, your long belly rises, the only one visible, the only one real in the whole cascade. Like caterpillars on hash, we give birth to words. Loving is the process of the night. This aching ink is made of the ashes of a thousand civilizations, cultures dead and continuing still; this borborial soil is where we begin. Like oil, words are life succumbed to time under pressure. Language is necrogenesis, and lover, that's no small death, though I do want you to come, in my arms to arrive like a green flash at sundown, and just as rare as obsidian spectacles. If you are ever ravished by lava—and what could surround you more?—you will at last remember what you really know in your breathless final seconds.

I don't remember what I said that night. We can only generalize and be approximately wrong. The kick from a shot of media is a convulsive sneeze, allergies, tics, divining Metatron flagellates.

Kathleen psighs, *It wasn't you; possession is nine-tenths of the Law.*

May the brightness never fall from your hair, I proquiesce.

Our eyes turn toward the fire as the darkness of Hilo gathers around us. Little blue and green flames lick and lap at the stream wood. Following the sparks upward we see the stars turning on in staggered sequence—emeralds, sapphires, rubies, diamonds and opals scattered about the sky in a puzzling, random distribution. Far beyond those galloping galaxies, or perhaps all too present to be seen, lurks the Mothership. The gaseous vertebrate.

They're filling the world with me now, her silence speaks to my eyes.

I let you go, I think. *I was an occident waiting to happen out here east of Eden. My heart was a broke-down engine, coughing, with smoke pouring out of a boxcar's mouth. But now we are found unto the west. Now I can hear all of you speak.*

We hardly knew what was happening to us, she replies, *I hardly knew you. Lay the leafage of years beside you—come close and kiss me again.*

And into me breathes a divine voice celebrating things

that shall be and things that were aforetime, and this voice urges me to sing the name of blessed Aquaknowledge that is both first and last.

Our telepathic link can jam the sux frequency. More devoted to each other than sky to the bosom of the air, you keep in your eyes the light of the star, in your hand the life line of your lover. The star has burned the curtain of the day, the flung traces of some distant molecule burst. We'll outstride the onslaught of alien televisuals with the memory of this moment. *Come on I wanna lay you*—your breasts, our lips, this peach, space is curved and time is relative. The mirror pool where we first became aware of our own images, indistinguishable, forever splitting apart, the fire-reflecting moon on the wind-rippled face of the water, inseparable, open-minded immunity, a telepathic catalyst which coalesces our souls together with the soul of the world. The images fill our desire—river, mountain, rose—it is the cusp to which we aspire. Urgone waves radiantly permeate us, the sane from eating the magic, the Aquaknowledge while rubbing the heresy, the flood of returning memories—*and break the kapu forever*.

Kathleen brushes my lips again, and all slips into silence. The city in ruins falls away to reveal the stream, and May is come again to its fecund banks. The great line of the centuries begins anew. Now the Virgin is reborn. Venus dons her crown of storied stars. Now a new generation ascends from the green earth, and our two-gathered voices join in a many-limbed song that choruses throughout the world.

Pied wind flowers and violets grow here, and daisies, these pearled Arcturi of the earth, the constellated flower that will never set. And in the warm hedge grow lush eglantine, green cowbind and the moonlight-colored may, and cherry blossoms, and white cups, whose wine is the bright dew, yet drained not by the day. And wild roses, and ivy serpentine, with dark buds and leaves wandering astray, and flowers azure, black, streaked with gold, fairer than any wakened eye may behold. And nearer to the water's edge grow broad flag flowers, purple, pranked with white, and starry river buds among the sedge, and floating water lilies, broad and bright. All is hued as if some great painter dips Her brush in the gloom of eruption and eclipse. Kathleen and I breathe deeply together, intentful desire unbroken.

○ ○ ○

Kathleen, Kathleen, behold your miracle.

You were ever more beautiful than the child becoming a woman could have ever imagined. I wanted to know your entire history, not only the story of your loves, your travels, the flight from Bali to Bombay, but the life you led before you found happiness, before the triumph. Your sad adolescence, thinking unceasingly of death, until by chance you one day entered a grocery store all aglitter with ads, and out of hatred for once being televised before a live audience, resolved that you would live.

It was years and years ago, when you were twenty-five, that a boy, a comet chaser, came along who loved to plunge his fingers into the dark fire of your hair. He left on a trip? Soon he will sleep, turned to marble, under the Southern Cross.

Wherever I was, you were in my mind and I did not quarrel. *All over all over again.*

○ ○ ○

At dawn, Kathleen and I surface to find the air thick with dread and portentous change, like just before a big blow. Hurricane's coming for to carry us away, and the cat is meowing, churning butter 'round my ankles.

"She wants us to follow her," Kathleen points out. I think I was just about to think that, but I can't seem to recall which way my buttons go.

"Scry?" the cat mewls, and that's when I remember.

"Did our link work?" I ask urgently, grasping her shoulders. "Did we break the sux?"

She grabs my hand and tugs me along.

"Let's go find out."

We walk hand in hand back towards Hilo. It stumps up around us, glowing sickly and smoking like an ancient emphysemic. And now I remember: this is the Open Mike gang clamoring with news.

∘ ∘ ∘

Just let him go, I hear a woman's voice cry. There are no aspirants for the igloo leaving next Wednesday, the job from hell. Chaotic carnival around a slave invasion, the sideshow freak Necks leap at our throats. Somebody has to do something, it's an automatic response. Implants litter the ground like popcorn, and we set Mrs. Lurie's clown on fire. The juggling trapeze artist gathers no moss, but my eyes are glued to the dead, black vid screen. Or maybe it's an old science fiction convention, with Nairbula as the ghost of honor. He was pulled up the sux but got spat out again, a little too gruff for the alien taste buds, or maybe the neighbor kids pulled him gasping from the burning pool, the aliens preferring a more homogenous cream off the top.

We all gather in the tension wires and prune our feathers for farthings while the ancient astronomer phlegms on about "alien indexes of indulgences" and "they're going to grant ours," *link worked*, "in the form of a sacrifice," at which mere mention we all whinny and nervously stamp our feet. "A sacrifice of sorts, more of a long-term hibernation, but he'll be allowed to receive mail," which seems strangely kind, but in a rocket nonetheless, though "more like a kite, really," Nairbula says. "Denny'll be flying a kite to the Flower World."

We don't believe our ears. The Flower World? What a

lunatic. Everything just stalls and stalls.

They just want one of us, these aliens with a pulsar twenty light-years away, but what's the limit of light among friends when the journey begins with the first step in his shoes?

J-Loop cries out, arguing that the aliens should make *her* fly the kite as she never really dies, and every woman who ever lived whose name began with J starts femifesting herself, orbiting around J-Loop's demand for justice.

Nairbula just stands there looking dismayed and confused. He doesn't realize that now people think he can negotiate with the aliens. He can't negotiate with a potassium-based life form: they're way too explosive. Fortunately, Margarine comes and leads him away.

"But wait," I yell after them, shoving through the crowd. "Wait!"

Finally they hear me. Nairbula stops and turns around. He seems startled to see me.

"You made it!" he says, genuinely amazed.

"Pardon?" I say, confused. Nairbula can't possibly know me, unless—

But who am I talking to? I feel sure I recognized this man's face just a moment ago.

"What did you want?" the old man asks me gently.

I shake my head, smile, shy at the traces. The top of my head is on fire, and the heat is slowly etching through my skull. Then I remember.

"What about the loRad, the bomb you left on the ship?"

Nairbula nods his head slowly and he doesn't stop. I don't think he recognizes me. Margarine whispers something in his ear. Nairbula shrugs.

"It didn't go off. Maybe they found it. All I know is what they told me before the sux collapsed. He'll be a little piece of psychic hardtack on the long sail home. Just a few crumbs per day, the minimum needed to stay alive.

This is their final judgment," Nairbula says.

After that, it is a long time before anything louder than a pin can be tolerated.

∘ ∘ ∘

Surcease, finally, from the flood of his disease, and he can see the end as he drifts, semiconscious, to sleep. Denny floats down the hall, waiting for the *in vitro* CEO of Infinite Star Systems to see him, to give him the news. The by-pass filter is working perfectly. He counts sheep while he waits. Tears stream down Scry's cheeks, flowing from the undiscovered country where lies the lost source of the Nile.

"...to some rathole of a planet in a galaxy far, far—"

"Denny."

"Yes?"

"Don't get carried away, baby. I refuse to think you'll be leaving the galaxy entirely."

"Right."

But they're not together. Denny's just dreaming so lucidly I can hear him on the cranial hemisphere bounce, scrabbling through the collapsed corridors and hallways of the Red King. *He can't hear you.* I'm waiting for the aliens to polybag and blast him into space, unless I can remember to do whatever it is I'm kicking myself for.

∘ ∘ ∘

Fuckwads demonstrating in front of alien ships!

Where is everybody? Where is Kathleen, I mean— Am I forgetting something? Just an earthbound misfit, I?

Fucking fundamentalists!

∘ ∘ ∘

What is this sensation? It's like what hollow metal—aluminum?—must feel. It might be reality sinking in. I feel I may have left some things out, or perhaps dwelt too long on unimportant particulars, but I remember the past few days quite clearly. I've been walking through the desert, heading for those distant hills hoarding the horizon. It's the bifurcatory strategy of convulsive psychology. I absorb all available evidence of every conceivable story, until I control the narrative, I call the shots.

I'm walking through the desert, and I've got my bomb. I don't really have control; I just have a dialogical bullet ricocheting through my mnemonic halls. Well, it's not a bomb, not in the killing or exploding sense. I may not know what the device does, though if I do it will come back to me. The device says her name is Ginja and that she wishes to send a signal into space. The hordes will be repelled with the Holy Hand Grenade of Alterity, a submission of such temerity it'll wrench the kiteworks into full reverse, killing negative thinking bugs dead.

I think she means to accompany me. *We are the signal.*

There will be no hob-nobbing with the denizens of the Flower World for Denny. Which would surely be lethal, hanging on a gas giant the temperature of Venus with a pulsar smacking up the sky. Just a little too much EM in the mix for the G-type bag we humans are in; the gravity alone would make gruelwork of him. So it would be a very short visit, one he would spend three hundred years making, unless Ginja could infiltrate the kite's navigational imperative and change the story. It's not a bomb; it's Scry's black virus cube. And I go in Denny's place.

∘ ∘ ∘

The peak of Rose Mountain isn't there; like any good mystic the mount long ago blew its top. The brain of rock is capillaried with lava tubes, fissures, sheets of connectivity. *This time I am the potassium,* I think. *Kathleen, if I don't meld with the mountain, we will live to love again.* I take a drink of water, a shot of golden seal, gather my meager memories, and leap.

The stars are obscured by smoke, and the smoke is lit from below by the flames injecting up from pools of molten glass. A man with a tin whistle piping wends through the alleys, nimbly skipping around puddles of mayhem. The surviving children follow behind, a straggling line of youths in various states of char rare.

"Hot wind coming," his whistle moans, and best they can, they all take cover. Immoral Thor swats the city, and a radioactive tumult of charged air gores the ruined metropolis like an angry bull struck by lightning. The noxious wind shreds, pushing bodies and wreckage before it, leaving in its wake a filthy, anxious sparkle, a shimmer that drips from jagged girder and bone like a stinking, liquid plastic.

"Come now!" cries the hailing whistle, and the children follow, hearts blazing with fear and hope. "Away! Away we go!"

Past the torn skirts of Hilo where refugees pillage and rampage with guns and gory stumps of arms only to stop and stare and face-wash with tears as the piper and children pass. Past the glowing, silky crater of the zoo, where a lone oryx joins the tattered line. Past the great highway that lies crumpled like eons of geologic faulting compressed into a few seconds. Past fissures that seethe with Earth's angry magma, past an unsinkable mountain that groans with memories of itself, past the flash-molded remains of a silicon implant factory, past, past all that.

"Come! We're almost there!" the whistle urgently coaxes. The piper stands quiet, just for a moment, on the lip of the biggest crater above which an Einsteinium-heavy warhead has consumed itself in entropic insanity. "Down we go to the bottom," trills the whistle, and the piper takes the first step.

And down they do go, unerringly, benumbed, into the miasma of fluorescing radiation. The last remaining strands of hair and clothing flame away, eyelids burn off, skin scorches and crinkles, the children survive silent in the mauling inferno.

"Quickly!" shrills the whistle, the piper marking time before a sheening door in the crater's pit, waiting for the children to tumble around him. Then a final, quick, supersonic arpeggio, and the subatomic revolving door begins to spin—

○ ○ ○

I am cocooned in an igneous kite, an obsidian arrowhead, jet black and transparent. I am floating high above the Earth, wafting and warbling in an atmosphere of uncertain distribution. Soon my tail will fan across the orbits of planets. I am stringed to the finger of an alien by a trail of broken memories.

I can see Denny, Scry, and Kathleen forming the three points of a stable plane on the ground below, and now supersymmetry is pulling us back apart, an ocean tiding my fate just like the salt water where we all started. I will take the shape of my container. I see Kathleen reach up into the air; she wants to stretch her slender loving arms way out into space, and I touch the fingers of her hands. I'm holding Scry's hand, too.

"Com'on," Denny says, squeezing palms. "We've got a lot of ground to cover."

After all our agricultural labor, after all the roads we've built, all the TV we've watched, the trio once again carries the light baggage of hunters and gatherers. Still, Kathleen lags behind, a hand on her belly.

"Come on, Kathleen. We really must keep moving. Cody's gone," Denny uses Kat's pet name for me. "There's nothing we can do about that."

"He'll be back," Scry says with a condensing that bellies through us all. But already I can feel the connection weakening with distance, like butter melting into its separate parts, and I don't know how far I have to go.

○ ○ ○

It's just you and me, Ginja, from here to the Flower World.

That's fine with me. That's exactly the kind of work I'm designed for. Eternal vigilance. Filter out all impurities. And on Earth, if you can't have sex, people go burnt on you and stick you out on guard duty on some goddess-forsaken crust of toast.

You can't have sex?

Look at me; I'm hyperdistributed. What are you going to do, impale yourself on my keyboard? Good luck. Fuck my ports? I don't think so.

But you get the concept; you could talk it through.

Interesting point, human. We'll have to run a few experiments.

There's just one problem.

What's that?

I'll be in knot space, asleep.

And I'll be in your dreams, and you'll be tuned to KOH.

Ricochet

ALL I HAVE TO DO IS THINK OF KOH, *Marco*, and let deus ex Ginja do the rest, *Polo*. I see the arrow of Ginja's intention fly by as she reaches out for the smuggled Baby loRad in the blaguey dungeons of the Mothership, throws everything in the pool. *Sux is up, suckers.* The rush from an injection, Ginja uncorks the zeroes and ones and blow it goes: no machine of loving grace, the Mothership explodes. The moon is a fire storm on the dark side, eclipsing the Earth. In the buffeting penumbra it is nothing but nanosecond after nanosecond of incandescent Tao. The moon begins to quake in two; every vine roars. *Say it three times.* We use our arms to hold the sacred. Together we reach, embrace the orb. The heart is faithful to the imaginal, and that is glue enough.

Our souls are made in collapsing stars, and consciousness precipitates like tears across the hot sky forever. A blue purie shoots through my brain. Suxed from the weakest thing, I ignite. The tying string snaps, and I am gone away from any longer holding back.

∘ ∘ ∘

I am the lips slumbering that do speak. I am the onomatopoeia of an orgasm, but I can't sleep until May is come and the green grass is grazed by an oryx. My name was Denny then. I had no idea I'd end up here, falling toward the Flower World, beating pulsar of a pollinated universe.

My body left behind, now I see him wavering through the dunes, one hand reining his camel. He left on a trip, and now he sleeps, turned to marble under the Southern Cross. Shrewder than a Chinese paintbrush, illness got the better of that black virgin he called his future. A lace of fins blows lightly over his great, mobile dream. Brother to fish, to seastars, to tentacled medusas, the scales no longer cold on his white belly. At the top of the sky his head is now the most precious of petrified sponges, and evanescent columns of air bubbles rise from his mouth, his nostrils, to the undulating roof of the waves.

An owl slaps me awake.

"Who do you think you are?"

○ ○ ○

Nairbula takes out his calculator, lets his fingers rest for a moment over the telescope's clock-drive interspace. As if he could grow any paler, but he does; he's becoming transparent.

There's a bear in the sky. Drown the book. One of the stars begins to move off and away—what is it? It is all an elaborate rose of some kind.

○ ○ ○

The spell of arms and voices—the black arms of roads, their promise of close embraces, and the telepathic arms of home worlds that stand beyond the moon, their tales of distant planets shimmering along the very fabric. They are held out to say: We are alone—come. And the voices say with them, "We are your people." And the air is thick with their company as they call to me, their kinsman, making ready to go, shaking the wings of their exultant and terrible age.

∘ ∘ ∘

The children shout and laugh on the long slope of hill, whole and healed, the dark pain forgotten. They run, blond and red and black and brown, and play in the deep green, soft, breeze-blown grass. They touch themselves and each other and smile. The wind is grace notes from a distant flute. The sun is fat and lazy. An oryx quietly grazes.

∘ ∘ ∘

Leave me now; I must be going. If I know someone for much longer than I've known you, I fall in love. When I am not braided into the text of this culture, I sometimes bubble to the surface of the mirror incomplete, and popping tension releases into the air—

You breathe me in the damp crescent of night, in a warm film on the plate glass of your seaward window—

You leave me now for a bus or a photography session. You pass now in explicitly split infinitives, a stream of people through a revolving door where we met that night—

Stay until the moon sets, at least. I am your lover until then. Rest between my pages like sinuous code, stain my covers with your golden seal root—

Flavored with essence, you are my opium. Taste, obsession and addiction lurk in the alleys of white space. Cuckolded by syntax, they are merely taunting shadows; given heat by heteroglossia, they ravish—

∘ ∘ ∘

Like a leopard through a fence ghostly you prowl the peripheries of my vision, vibrating the dust that's lain on these panes for years, the kaleidoscope collection so ancient the bits of glass have flown together like birds refined from ash. Once a year when the light strikes the grimy porthole just right, a ray swims across the black glass cabin and refracts itself in a sagan's number of liquid colors, escaping prismers telling tales of taking Chiron's ferry home. Like slow sand, over time, meaning collapses and collects in a pool at its own feet. Who narrates the history of windows?

∘ ∘ ∘

I ache because I have no idea of what is real; all is coincidence and contradiction. I hear that we're each unique, but I have to take the word of those who've come before on that. I'm floundering in a soup of stimuli that could be real or that I could be making up or that could be nothing at all, just dream televisions blaring from the corners of the world, broadcast radiation captured by the cupped ears of alien antennæ. My thoughts continue to lead me astray, bite my own tail—let me ring with the power of your harmonics, thrill to the glissando trill from your flute hovering over my basso continuoso, punctuate me with your ruffle of snares and turnings of prayer wheels. The dream had me, not I the dream. For you, I will wash my hands with hope, scrub away every experience, good, bad or indifferent, and start all over again. In the labyrinth of our parting, open me like Theseus's thesaurus, and speak the many alternatives to these words.

Author photo by Nancy Casey

Clark currently lives in Northern Idaho. He has been an independent literary publisher and editor, short order cook, glyphic designer, and hermetic ordealist. This is his first novel.